CUTTHROAT DOGS

CUTTHROAT DOGS

An Amos Walker Novel

Loren D. Estleman

A Tom Doherty Associates Book
New York

CUTTHROAT DOGS

Copyright © 2021 by Loren D. Estleman

All rights reserved.

A Forge Book
Published by Tom Doherty Associates
120 Broadway
New York, NY 10271

www.tor-forge.com

Forge® is a registered trademark of Macmillan Publishing Group, LLC.

The Library of Congress Cataloging-in-Publication Data is available upon request.

ISBN 978-1-250-25865-6 (hardcover)
ISBN 978-1-250-25864-9 (ebook)

Our books may be purchased in bulk for promotional, educational, or business use. Please contact your local bookseller or the Macmillan Corporate and Premium Sales Department at 1-800-221-7945, extension 5442, or by email at MacmillanSpecialMarkets@macmillan.com.

First Edition: January 2022

Printed in the United States of America

0 9 8 7 6 5 4 3 2 1

In memory of Millie Puechner: Thrust simultaneously into literary agency and stepmotherhood, she brought honor to both with peerless efficiency and boundless love.

CUTTHROAT DOGS

ONE

'd been arrested before, of course; in my line of work, having to make bail on occasion is a kind of business tax.

The department had worked innovations since the last time. A youngster who looked less like a cop than a pharmacist's apprentice asked me politely to place my palms flat on a sheet of gray tempered glass. Something hummed and a beam of light swept the glass from side to side, recording my prints electronically and without ink.

I looked at my unstained fingers. "I'll be damned."

Officer Rexall had an infectious grin. "I know, right? Paid for itself the first month just in what we saved on Kleenex."

I placed my free call in Receiving, with a cop standing by pretending not to eavesdrop; this one looked like a desk sergeant in a sitcom, blowfish-faced and bored half to death. For once Barry Stackpole answered on the second ring. He'd recognize the police number on caller ID. At this point in his odyssey through the techno-wilderness, he was hosting a podcast on the theme of organized crime and domestic terrorism. When I introduced myself, he asked what I'd been pinched for this time.

"Driving in the bus-only block on Woodward. They're cracking down. You got any contacts left in print journalism?"

"One or two, if their livers are still functioning. Shouldn't you be calling a lawyer?"

"What for? The cops already emptied my pockets. I want a re-porter, a photographer, and Page One of the City section in the *News* and *Free Press*. You can't buy this kind of advertising."

What happened was this:

I've always had a laissez-faire attitude toward bank robbery. Now that the banks have laid off all the armed guards, eliminated teller's cages, and order the employees not to offer resistance to criminals, what's to stop you? Just send your gun and the note with your demands by way of the pneumatic tube in the drive-through and the cashier will send the money and return the weapon by the same route. Insurance covers the depositors. As long as you don't intend to hurt anyone, why *not* rob a bank?

This character broke the rules.

It was in the downtown office of the Detroit Bank & Trust Building. I'd stopped trying to keep up with all the corporate aliases it had gone through since local tags went obsolete, so I still called it by its original name. It's a lodestone of 1960s architec-ture: twenty-eight stories of tinted windows shaped like a box of shredded wheat.

I pegged him standing three spots ahead of me in line. His right hand stayed out of sight inside the zipper briefcase under his left arm and he turned his head away from the counter every fifteen seconds, just as the surveillance camera rotated his direction. He wore a rust-colored suede jacket, jeans, blazing white Ree-boks, long curly hair, and a droopy moustache. All his fashion and grooming tips seemed to come from 1970s porn films.

It didn't have anything to do with me, even if his hand came out of that case holding anything more lethal than the standard-issue note implying he was armed. Felons these days are getting to be bashful about brandishing weapons.

The game changed when his turn came and he leveled a Glock

Nine at the pretty blonde behind the counter and shouted, "Gimme the cash, now!"

That tore it.

I don't approve of people raising their voices in public, especially when they're threatening someone with a gun. It's redundant. I waited until the customers cleared from the line of fire, shouting and stumbling over one another, then slipped the Chief's Special from my kidney holster and shot him in the leg.

I hit the bone that sticks out at the side of the knee. It's the most painful place you can inflict an injury, and he hit the floor hard. His pistol sprang from his hand and scraped along the tile floor, spinning like a bottle. I made two long strides and kicked it into the far corner.

Alarms were clanging by this time, one in the bank, another in the nearest precinct house. The man I'd shot was still trying to rise, his gun hand clasping his bleeding leg, when the first siren ground down in front of the building and the uniforms came boiling in, pistols and riot guns raised. He was so pale now his wig and paste-on moustache stood out like the cheap Halloween costume it was. I just had time to let go of my .38 and throw up my hands before the cops tackled me. Of course I was the first one cuffed.

The blue-and-white they piled me into smelled like a urinal cake. It took a radio call from Dispatch and made a U-turn in the middle of Congress. I'd heard the instructions.

"Why the Second?" I said. "That's Homicide. I just nicked his knee."

The cop in the front passenger's seat, light brown with dark freckles, told me to shut the fuck up.

Minutes later we swung into the small lot belonging to a low brick building that looked like a junior high school. Inside, a cross-section of the community sat in a row of orange plastic chairs, some bored, some fretful, like classroom cut-ups waiting to see the vice principal. The room was crowded with uniforms and hip guns. So far it still looked like school.

After I'd made my call to Barry, Sergeant Blowfish took me by the arm and led me in another unexpected direction. I'd hung around the Second Precinct often enough to know where the holding cells were. He took me down a different hall to a door I'd never been through, with an empty slot on the wall next to it where a nameplate was supposed to go. I knew the voice that answered his knock better than I knew my own.

My escort opened the door and gave me a gentle push. "Walker, Inspector."

John Alderdyce sat behind a painted plywood desk reading a printed sheet. He shooed the sergeant on out and tipped a palm toward another orange plastic chair on my side of the desk. I took it and watched him take off his glasses. That brought out the jagged features of his Lego-built face. Whoever had assembled it hadn't bothered with the finer details; he'd just stretched black skin over it and split.

"You know what the penalty is for carrying a handgun into a bank in the state of Michigan?"

"You get shot by me."

"A five-thousand-dollar fine and a year in prison. When you get out, you won't have an investigator's license."

"Are you sure you can yank it? Officially you're retired from the department."

"Not anymore. The chief confirmed my consultant's position last week. You're my first case."

"Starting slow, aren't you? The pip-squeak who printed me could've done it."

"You only got him because I had Dispatch re-route you to this precinct when I caught the squeal. You were on your way to Robbery Armed. *Officially*"—he stressed the word—"we could book you for intent to commit armed robbery on the evidence, and change the charge later; if we wanted to."

"Until that Glock came out I forgot I had the damn thing on me. I just came off a security job and went in to deposit the check."

"You forgot. Well, that changes everything."

"You're sarcastic, I can tell."

He waited.

I rolled a shoulder. "I'm pretty sure he was hopped up, the way he was yelling. A live cashier has to count for something."

He glanced down at the sheet on the desk and signed it, leaning back to see what he was doing without putting his readers back on. Then he slid it into a letter tray. "Why do you think I stole you out from under Pollard at R/A? He sleeps with a copy of the department manual under his pillow and he's got a hard-on against rental heat. That sheriff's star you carry would be an extra piece of candy in his piñata. It's a clear violation."

"I'd junk it, only it opens some doors."

"Personally I'd rather live with the case of hives I get knowing you're walking around flipping off the law than risk an uptick in the homicide rate; but I'm getting to be in the minority. We're in the showcase-bust business now: Sweep 'em in the front door, sweep 'em out the back. I'm jeopardizing my brand-new job first step out of the gate. You never know what side of the bed this chief woke up on today. I'm thinking of hedging my bet: Tank you on the weapons beef and put in a word with the county prosecutor, get you probation as a first offender. Then again, you never know what side *she* got up on."

"It seems to be a contagious condition."

"Nuh-uh. I had a good mood going until about an hour ago."

Voices clamored outside the door. A vein throbbed in my temple. Only one segment of the population argued with authority in quite that tone.

"Jesus!" Alderdyce's perpetual scowl spread to his hairline.

"The press in this town can smell a byline like a bitch in heat. How the hell did they know we brought you here?"

I hoped the question was rhetorical. That spur-of-the-moment idea I'd had was beginning to look less like a stroke of genius and more like just a stroke. The Tuesday night special at County was a Band-Aid on a cracker.

Still glowering, he picked up his glasses, tapped a corner on the desk a few times, then dropped them again. He slid open a drawer, took out my wallet, ID folder containing the illegal county shield, keys, and the Smith & Wesson in its belt clip, and placed them on my side of the desk.

"Just make sure you tell them how fast we responded."

"Made me proud of my city." I put everything away and fled the scene.

TWO

The papers got the hero angle before TV. The police withheld the surveillance footage twenty-four hours, so there was no art, which determined the amount of play any story received, and the camera trucks went to Robbery Armed first. The stand-up talent didn't know there was a twist, so they didn't ask, and of course the department spokesman there didn't volunteer it. You couldn't blame him: The cops had their man in jig time, a rare enough event to shout over the airwaves and skip some details. The bank was closed; the witnesses the reporters managed to reach at home gave confused accounts of what happened. You couldn't blame them, either: They were all ducking for cover and from start to finish my part of the show ran less than a minute.

My press conference closed too late to make the print deadline, so bright and early the next day I went out and snagged a copy of the *Free Press*. My face sneered at me from the first page of Section B. I was misquoted, the reporter got the make and model of my weapon wrong, and the bullet that clipped the bandit's left knee made a detour and struck him in the right thigh. Which was okay, because that's what I was aiming for in the first place.

Everything else was pretty much as it happened, although if you've ever been present at a newsworthy event and read about it later, you remember it seemed to belong to someone else's story.

The robber's name was Everett. He'd served two tours in

Afghanistan with Army Special Forces and received a medical discharge. Three doctors had diagnosed him with post-traumatic stress syndrome. He was an insanity plea waiting to happen. I didn't care. I'd lost interest in him the second I kicked away his gun.

As for me, I looked grayer than I did in the mirror, and my chiseled features looked as if they'd been carved in butter, but they got my name and profession right. So did the *News* that afternoon, along with an old photo from the library, with the inmate number cropped out. Barry's former employer must have been nursing a grudge ever since his ace columnist left for the twenty-first century, so he didn't send a photographer. Anyway, the account that accompanied a younger, even more peevish-looking champion of justice ran closer to fact. All I had to do was wait, holding a bucket to catch all the job offers.

It might have worked, too, if a minivan driver hadn't turned on his radio in time for God to order him to jump the curb and crush six pedestrians on Griswold during the noon rush hour. I found that out the evening after my Superman act, when Channel Four opened with the story. All I'd known was I got a call from the station apologizing for canceling my interview at the last minute for a late-breaking story: Same thing from Two and Seven on voice mail while I was on the line.

Even so, I expected some celebrity to stick. Rosecranz, the troll who changed the lightbulbs in my office building—beginning with a free sample from Tom Edison—approached me with a baggy grin when I entered the lobby the next morning. I braced myself to accept sloppy praise. Instead he announced he'd changed the lock on my door, and handed me a pair of keys linked with a twist-tie. I'd put in my order three years ago, after someone broke in and ripped the plumbing out of my water closet for scrap. Then I remembered he'd given up on learning to read English and the only thing he ever watched on TV was men wrestling bears on a Russian-language channel.

Some calls did come in. The phone was ringing when I unlocked the door to my private office. I fed the keys to the dead rhododendron in its pot and leaned across the desk to pick up.

A wobbly falsetto voice said, "Is that Amos Walker, the scourge of pirates, road agents, slave traders, and the heartbreak of psoriasis?"

I gave Barry Stackpole some advice of an anatomical nature and banged the receiver into the cradle.

He'd call back. I settled myself into the swivel and started to take the phone off the hook. Then I remembered why I'd passed up a chance to call a lawyer and lit a cigarette, killing time before it rang again and hoping it wasn't who I knew it would be.

It rang. When I heard his natural voice I said, "You know most of the population doesn't know what the heartbreak of psoriasis means. It's almost before *my* time."

"I read the room first. How many clients you got lined up, and when can I expect my fifteen percent as your press agent?"

"You can have it right now. You're the first to call, not counting a cremation service in Highland Park."

"Highland Park *is* cremation. Seriously, doesn't anyone follow the news anymore? Apart from Facebook and Comedy Central?"

"Nope. It makes me feel a little less lonely. Who'd've thought obsolescence would turn out to be cutting-edge?"

"Cheer down. Your incessant perkiness is making me pre-diabetic."

"Who's a guy got to shoot in the knee to get attention?"

"The president; but you'd better move fast. And *that* news cycle's liable to be shorter than yours."

The phone rang ten seconds after I hung up.

"A. Walker Investigations."

"You the guy shot that robber?" This was a gravelly voice; a smoker's cough capable of speech.

"That's me."

"My wife's trying to poison me."

"How do you know?"

"She used to be a good cook. Lately everything she makes tastes like Styrofoam."

We wasted three minutes working it out. She'd switched to a gluten-free diet and had dragged him along to simplify things in the kitchen.

"A. Walker Investigations."

"Are you the man—?" A woman this time, young from the sound.

"Yeah, in the knee. Unless you read the *Free Press*."

"I don't read newspapers. I heard it on talk radio."

"I didn't know I'd cracked that wall. What can I do for you?"

"I want you to speak to my Civics class at Wayne State on a citizen's responsibility to the community. I need the extra credit."

"A. Walker Investigations."

"Is this—?" A man with a southern urban accent.

"How can I serve you?"

"My next door neighbor's a murderer. I want you to catch him."

I sat forward and ground out my cigarette stub in the ashtray. "Are you sure?"

"I saw the whole thing."

"What did you see?"

"It was a hit-and-run, right in front of my house. She's dead there in the street. I love her and he killed her." The voice broke.

"Did you call the police?"

"I did! They said there's nothing they can do!"

I dragged over a pad and took a pencil out of the cup. "What's your friend's name?"

"Fluffy."

That kind of thing continued off and on for the rest of the day. I turned down divorce work twice, referred one caller to a lawyer, got into a fight with a man who wanted me to beat someone up, and took down contact information on a couple of possibles-but-unlikelies. I was headed out for home when the phone rang for the last time. I almost didn't answer it.

"Is this Mr. Walker?"

This was another young female, nearly inaudible.

"Yes, it is."

"I wanted to thank you for saving my life in the bank."

I cocked a hip up onto the corner of the desk. "You're the cashier?"

"I—I haven't been into work since. The manager's a nice man. He said I didn't have to come in until I was ready, and I'd still be paid. Everyone's been so kind, even the reporters; most of them, anyway."

"Sweet of them. You might've been killed."

"I heard you were arrested."

"I expected to be. It's routine. It turned out all right. The police dropped the charges. Are you okay?"

"I'm not sure. I held up until I got home, then I fell apart. Like after an accident?"

"Me, too. Shooting at someone and getting shot at are just about the same. It was very nice of you to call. Is there anything I can do for you?"

"Yes!"

I almost fell off the desk. It came that quickly and with such certainty.

"Someone is dead who shouldn't be, and the wrong man is in prison."

I was silent. Then she spoke again.

"Can we meet?"

THREE

They say we're living in the post-modern age; that, according to the banner stretched across the front of the building, was the name of the exhibit taking place at the Detroit Institute of Arts. Maybe someday our language will make as much sense as a jump-rope rhyme.

I was early, so I killed time in the foyer, admiring Diego Rivera's mural wrapped around all four walls glorifying assembly-line laborers at work in the Ford River Rouge plant, popping their biceps and baring their teeth in concentration. Ford had replaced them with robots, and soon also the drivers of the automobiles built there. My own redundancy was getting to be contagious.

We'd agreed on the location because it was the middle of the week, the weather was grim, and hardly anyone downtown cares to swim through drizzling rain in order to spend his lunch hour looking at bent sheets of copper on pedestals and yards of colored cloth pinned up on walls; the same went double out in the neighborhoods. It's as private a place to conduct sensitive business as any in our zip code. Also admittance is free.

Five minutes before eleven the morning after we'd spoken, I reported to the cafeteria, where I spotted her at one of the few occupied tables. She looked older than she had behind the bank counter, but at a certain point in their twenties, most people look younger with a gun pointed at them. Past thirty, given the same circumstances, they age by the second.

At that she was young enough to make a vintage heart ache; twenty-five at the outside, an ash-blonde who wore her hair straight to the shoulders with leftward-sweeping bangs—Mary Travers of Peter, Paul and Mary style—a strong straight nose, and a diamond-shaped face set squarely on a long neck. Her eyes were set wide and she appeared to be wearing no makeup of any kind, which meant she knew how to apply it. Her coral-colored boat-neck top displayed her collarbone to advantage. I'm a pushover for a well-formed clavicle.

"Christine?"

She jumped. She'd been looking away as I approached. A cloud of fear scudded past the diamond-shaped face. Then she focused on me. "Chrys, actually; with a *y*." She spoke as low as she had on the phone, but there was no straining to hear. Her voice was as clear as a glass chime.

"That's unusual." I slid into the chair facing her.

"It's short for Chrysanthemum." A slight flush replaced the cloud. "My parents were neo-hippies."

"I'm paleo myself. You're not eating?" There was nothing in front of her on the table.

"I don't do breakfast."

"We're going to get along. Coffee or tea?"

"Coffee, please." She unslung a shoulder bag from the back of her chair, black with a yellow metal clasp.

"My treat," I said. "How do you take it?"

She smiled. I knew there was one in there someplace. "Neat."

"Better yet." I got up, went away, and came back lugging two steaming ivory mugs. She tasted hers and made a face.

I nodded. "Art students come in sometimes to copy the old masters. I think they use these cups to mix their paints."

She lifted her shoulders and let them drop. There was something Gallic in the movement. Her last name was Corbeil. "As long as it's hot."

"That's the spirit. I saw your interview on Fox. You handled yourself well."

"You didn't see what they did to me on Channel Seven. They started to rearrange all my furniture to lay their cables. They broke a glass. When I told them to stop they said I was violating the First Amendment. I said, 'Let's call the police and see who they arrest.' At eleven o'clock all they showed was me slamming the door in their faces."

"And you thought the gun part was the worst."

Her expression went dead. "It was."

"Sure it was. I was trying to cheer you up. That's what we paleo-hippies do."

Her smile this time was obligatory; not much more than a tic. She slid the mug to one side and leaned forward, folding her arms on the table. Her tone fell almost to a whisper, but still it came through clearly. "You said on the phone our conversation would be confidential."

"It is."

"How can I be sure?"

I scratched a number on the back of one of my cards and slid it across the table, along with the pen. "That's John Alderdyce's direct line. He's a special consultant to the Detroit Police Department with the rank of inspector. He'll tell you what it's like to fish in my pond. It won't be complimentary. Keep the pen," I said. "I've got a drawerful back at the office. I swiped this one off his desk day before yesterday."

She picked up the ballpoint and looked at it. It was dark blue, with DETROIT POLICE DEPARTMENT printed on it in gold. She hauled a satchel-size handbag up from the floor and took out a phone. After bouncing it on her palm a couple of times she put it back, lowered the bag, and laid the pen on top of the card.

"Okay. I've got an older brother, and I mean older; he was grown and off to college before I was two. That's where he was arrested."

"Where's that?"

"University of Detroit. He was studying drafting. He chose a Catholic school over Michigan, so he could study cathedrals. His chief interest was in Gothic and Romanesque architecture. Albert Kahn was his hero. You know Kahn?"

"Hard not to, in this town."

"I didn't. Since then I've had a crash course, thanks to Dan. That's his name, Dan Corbeil."

"Short for Dandelion?"

"No, he came along before Woodstock Two, where our folks were converted. I never got to know him well until recently. By the time I was old enough to form a real impression, he was in prison in Jackson."

"You said someone's dead who shouldn't be. Does that mean your brother's in for murder?"

"Yes. You might have heard about it. A girl was found dead in the bathtub in her apartment off the U of D campus. She was a freshman. Dan was a junior. They'd been going out for some time, so of course his fingerprints were all over the place. The police kept at him until he stumbled all over his answers."

"They do that. They don't need rubber hoses anymore. They've all taken psych classes. Some of them could make Saint John the Baptist plead to serial rape, through a combination of persistence and the power of suggestion. A good lawyer can get that kind of evidence thrown out of court on the basis of duress."

"Our parents were sure his innocence was enough. They hired a public defender, straight out of law school. Dan's been locked up for nineteen years."

"Where'd he go after the state closed Jackson?"

"The Huron Valley Men's Correctional Facility, in Ypsilanti."

"Uh-huh."

She jerked up her chin. "What?"

"Don't read too much into it. There have been incidents that could've been avoided, but that's what happens when you pay the guards minimum wage. Most places do. HVMC's no worse than most. It's a long way from a hell hole."

"Depends on your definition of hell. I'm terrified for him."

"Has he had trouble with the officers or his fellow inmates?"

"He hasn't said; but I don't think that's it. I've been seeing him every visiting day for years. He was gaining weight at first, the way I'm told some do, from lack of real exercise and eating those fatty foods they serve to keep them too out of shape to make an escape attempt, but lately he's been wasting away. I—I think he's planning on killing himself."

"Say anything specific?"

She shook her head. "It's just a feeling I got. He used to put some effort into sounding positive—for me, I mean, so I wouldn't worry—but now he seems not to care. That's got to be some kind of sign, don't you think?"

"I don't know," I said. But I did.

I drank from the mug and set it down as carefully as Viennese crystal; stalling for thought. "You said you didn't really get to know him till recently. Are you sure you know him now? Inmates get more practice than the rest of us at making an impression favorable to their case. I've been to parole hearings and seen it firsthand."

"No!" She said it loudly enough to draw attention from the other diners. Compared to her usual ultra-quiet speech she might have been bellowing. She clenched her fists, turning down the volume by force. "Maybe you'll understand if you know the victim's name. It's the April Goss murder, Mr. Walker; twenty years ago."

"Ah." I sat back.

FOUR

The April Goss murder was a sleeper. First reported as a suicide, then an unsolved murder in a week of heavier-than-usual carnage, it took on stature in direct proportion to the twists and turns in the evidence, along with the amount of attention brought to it in the legal arena.

On a typically raw, gusty morning in mid-March, a fellow female student living across the hall entered Goss's unlocked apartment to find the tenant sprawled naked in a tub full of water, tinged pink with her blood; both wrists were slashed and the posterior tibial artery was nicked behind one knee. Complete desanguination would have taken place in a couple of hours, well after the victim had drifted into unconsciousness. Warm water and a slow trickle; it was the McDonald's menu-meal choice of most suicides. When a background check discovered that she'd been diagnosed bipolar and prescribed anti-depressant drugs, that initial impression seemed confirmed.

Then the forensics team filed its report.

The room was on the second floor of a house on Livernois not far from the university, the ugly brainchild of a stoveworks baron of the Taft era with tons of business sense and not an ounce of taste. It had been off-campus student housing for decades. April Goss's was a studio apartment, once a child's schoolroom. It was there the original theory started to go sour.

Smudges on the bloodstained razor blade resting on the edge of the tub might or might not have been the victim's; it's rare to lift a print off one that would pass a coroner's inquest. But even the most fastidious self-destructive types didn't wipe their doorknobs their last time through. The ones on the hallway and bathroom doors contained only those left by the neighbor who'd discovered the body. Then the specialist who'd identified Goss's condition reported that after three years on mild anti-depressants and a trial period without, the patient demonstrated no symptoms of bipolar disorder; not an unusual occurrence among young adults.

"Teenage angst," he was quoted, shaking his head. "Like acne, most outgrow it."

Whether or not the doctor remembered his own adolescence with any clarity, his statement on top of the physical evidence made the case homicide. After the girl from next door was cleared of any possible motive, the investigation proceeded to the next likely suspect: the boyfriend.

In every investigation, there's an outward silence while the detectives run down every spore; but in our microwave, Instagram, zip-and-seal society, patience is on life support. Goss's father, a mid-level executive with some local media company, and her mother, a legal secretary, pressed for action, through the hellcat attorney Mrs. Goss worked for. He was a high-profile character who ran advertising on all the local TV stations throughout prime-time, a snarling, cage-rattling predator based on his image, taped on courthouse steps cherry-picking questions from squads of on-air personalities; so of course there was an arrest in short order.

Forensics had bagged an empty box from a home pregnancy kit in Goss's bathroom wastebasket, along with a treated plastic stick that according to the instructions turned blue when urinated on by an expectant mother. It was blue, and the first impression was that this supported the suicide scenario; when that collapsed, Dan Corbeil became a suspect. When it comes to motives, cops love the Big Three: Fear, greed, and wrath, simple emotions you can sell a jury without confusing it with a lot of explanation. Nothing frightens a young man on the cusp of a promising future like the prospect of being tied down with a family.

An autopsy turned up trace amounts of Seconal in the corpse, and a bottle with her doctor's name on the label. It was the same doctor who'd treated her earlier; he told detectives she was an insomniac, and since she'd tested clear of bipolar, he considered it safe to prescribe a low dosage of the sedative. While the amount in her system wasn't sufficient to put her out entirely, she'd ingested enough to make it difficult to put up a fight. Anyone of ordinary strength could have overpowered her, stripped her, placed her in the tub, and made the fatal cuts, holding her down until she was too weak to climb out.

Dan Corbeil had been seeing Goss for several months. According to the witness who'd found her body, there were no other men in her life. He didn't help his case when he said he'd been pulling an all-nighter with a study group at the time of her death. The other members of the group admitted they'd been drinking and smoking pot, and everyone was too wasted to say just when Corbeil left. With no one to support his alibi, and enough medical training to know which veins to pierce, he was arrested and charged with murder.

He swore she'd said nothing to him about even taking the test, but after fudging about his activities at the time of her death, his testimony on the stand fell apart under cross-examination. The jury took less than three hours to convict.

The kicker was she wasn't pregnant. The autopsy confirmed that. The packages containing home pregnancy test products all carry warnings of false positives; but neither Goss nor Corbeil could know the truth.

"It's circumstantial," I said, when Chrys Corbeil finished bringing me up to speed on the twenty-year-old investigation; "but then most murder cases are, even the smoking guns. Nothing makes a cop happier than when somebody decides to get cute and rig a crime scene to look like something else. They've seen the same TV shows."

"The—cops—seemed happy, that's for sure," she said.

"You've talked with them?"

"My parents did, when they tried to bail him out. Of course that was out of the question, and they knew it, but they never stopped talking about how pleased the—the cops—were that they'd tied everything up so soon, with a big white bow. They gave no thought to Eric and Elaine, or even the poor Goss girl, as human beings; they were just pieces in a game, the way patients are just gall bladders and compound fractures to surgeons."

"Eric and Elaine?"

"Our parents. They insisted we call them by their first names. They considered *Mom* and *Dad* 'emblems of patriarchal-matriarchal slavery.' Their words."

"I'm getting a real picture of them."

"Don't jump to conclusions, Mr. Walker. They were good people. They taught us right from wrong. That's one of the reasons I know Dan didn't kill anyone."

"It's also the legal language for rejecting a plea of insanity. If killers never knew right from wrong, the prisons would have rooms to rent."

But her upbringing explained something I'd noticed earlier: her hesitation in using the word *cops*. It was almost spinsterish. I could picture dear Eric and Elaine batting around words like "fuzz" and "pigs"; self-consciously, being second-generation flower children: kids trying on grown-up words the way an earlier generation stole cigars and smoked them behind the barn.

Then again, that was too much to try to get out of one phrase dropped into the middle of a few minutes' acquaintance.

She'd lapsed into a sullen silence. I said, "You said they *were* good people. They're dead?"

"My mother is. Her doctor said it was from an accidental combination of sleeping pills and alcohol. My father—"

"Seconal?"

"No!" More heads turned. Her hands on the table were clenched into fists. Her throat worked as she tamped herself down. "No," she said, in her usual tone. "It was over-the-counter. Personally I'm not sure it was accidental. I'm not sure it was deliberate, either; maybe a little of both. Dan was twelve years into a life sentence. By then she'd lost all hope."

"What about your father?"

"I don't know where he is. He didn't come home after the funeral, just left all his stuff in the house. I was sixteen. It was all too much for him or he'd never have done it; but he didn't leave me stranded. All our names were on my parents' joint savings account. When months passed and he hadn't touched it, I began drawing on it. With that and a string of jobs I paid my bills, finished high school, and put myself through college: Wayne State."

"Must've been a pretty good chunk to start."

"My parents were partners in a hydroponics farm they founded. In ten years they made enough to sell the business and retire on their investments in sustainable energy corporations; Dan's and my names were on those accounts too. They don't pay as well as they once did, but my salary at the bank covers the rent. I can pay your fee, if it's not unreasonable."

I sidestepped that for the time being. "Eric and Elaine did right by you, despite what happened at the end. I don't just mean what they left you."

"I'll take that as a compliment."

I sipped coffee. It was lukewarm. I'd forgotten it was there. I pushed away the cup and rested my forearms on the table. "There are organizations that specialize in reopening old investigations. Have you tried that route?"

"The ones that bothered to look into it weren't encouraging. They cited the reason all of Dan's requests for an appeal were denied. There was nothing wrong with the procedure in the courtroom, you see." Her fists on the table were as tight as square knots.

"That's the system. In real life, Dr. Richard Kimble would've had to jump through a couple of dozen hoops to get his conviction reversed, even after he'd found the one-armed man."

The lunch rush, or what passed for it, was over; we were the last ones still seated. The bussers were getting busy and a vacuum cleaner whined across the room. I told her my day rate and what I needed up front; I didn't know if it was reasonable, but I don't own shares in eco-friendly corporations or any other. She frowned, doing the math in her head like a good cashier. Then she winched the handbag back up onto her lap, took out a checkbook bound in black imitation leather, and picked up the pen from the police department.

FIVE

hilip Justice was the name of the attorney the Gosses had engaged to put the screws to the police investigating April's murder; some dim ancestor had been granted the surname by European royalty for his success in chasing horse-drawn ambulances. "Rough Justice" (the line decorated every bus in town) was too tall, too loud, and had won most of his decisions by making a nuisance of himself in court. His firm still advertised on local TV, racking up totals earned for its clients in big fat numerals followed by strings of zeroes, but the man himself was gone, a victim of one of the very people he represented; tossed aside like a chicken bone once he'd served his purpose. I'd been within yards of him at the time. Since then I'd made it a point not to stand too close to a lawyer in the open.

After saying good-bye to Chrys Corbeil in the DIA I crossed Woodward Avenue to the main branch of the Detroit Public Library, a marble pile that might have been deliberately designed to frighten away anyone who wanted to use it; but I was on a first-name basis with the vagrants who slept at the carrels, so it was like dropping in at the club for brandy and a cigar. A couple of hours scrolling through ancient numbers of the *News* and *Free Press* on microfilm didn't put me much further ahead on the details of the murder and the trial that followed, but I recognized an acquaintance in one of the pictures taken at the crime scene.

That was no treat.

Stan Kopernick had taken on girth and some gray hairs since swapping his uniform for plainclothes, but no one would have called him callow even then. He'd looked like a beefier, swarthier version of Dick Tracy, poured into starched blues and left to set. The photographer had posed him pointing at the tub from which the victim had been removed and identified him in the caption by name as an officer with the Eleventh Precinct. Neither the shot nor Kopernick's presence was necessary, but probably he'd leaked details of the investigation in return for the plug. Face-time wins points with the front office. The more often a particular grunt shows up in the news, the more inclined the department brass is to credit it to hard work and efficiency. Pretty soon he's on the fast track to the CID.

It isn't even corrupt, really. Any public service is a sieve, and the organization keeps an entire division to spin sensitive information into good public relations, or release enough false leads to bury anything that would hinder the investigation. The local media were aware of it, but all they cared about was the next news cycle. Even so, it increases the possibility of putting someone in a position of power who'd be better employed stunning cattle. Detective First-Grade Kopernick was a case in point.

I had a personal interest, that's all; no one can clean up the system all by himself. My track record with him since he'd joined Major Crimes was untidy, to put it delicately. He wouldn't go out of his way to break me in two, but if the opportunity presented itself he'd be on it like bruises on a banana. He was just what I needed to spice up the prospect of reopening an old case the police had shut with a bang.

Going over his head would be a fine way to give him his chance.

It was a warm day in late April, just the kind to make the trees bud before the frost. I groped for a signal on the library steps and called the Second Precinct.

The voice I got was youthful enough to belong to the officer who'd printed me; even desk sergeants have to take bathroom breaks. He told me Inspector Alderdyce wasn't in today.

"Out sick?"

"He only comes in three days a week. He'll be here tomorrow."

I thanked him, hit End, and was halfway through pecking out Alderdyce's home number when I changed my mind. I'm not man enough to risk antagonizing two cops at the same time. I was already on John's list for inviting the press in on my arrest; you don't get that far up the ladder—twice, the second time after coming out of retirement—without developing a keen nose for a double-cross. I canceled the call.

Next I dug out my smudged notebook and looked up the number of the Huron Valley Men's Correctional Facility in Ypsilanti to find out if the visiting hours were still the same as last time.

It's an old town, named for the Greek revolutionary leader, with rows of crazy-quilt Victorian houses built by lumber kings and railroad barons, a picturesque Depot Town filled with pubs and architectural salvage shops, Eastern Michigan University's green and ivy-grown campus, bookstores that buy and sell used school texts, a Masonic temple, and one of the worst crime districts in the state. Institutions of justice like police stations and penitentiaries attract the worst neighbors; it has something to do with the notion that such locations are psychological No-Man's Zones. The men's correction house fronted on Bemis Road, announcing itself blocks ahead with signs warning motorists not to pick up hitch-hikers; especially those in denim jumpsuits with homemade tattoos carved into their arms.

It doesn't look like the medieval dungeons in prison flicks. They exist, but from a time before the system began hiring contractors uninfluenced by Traitors' Gate. This one resembles a modern-day hospital, with the bricks pre-stacked in orderly cubes lowered into place by cranes and the bars discreetly camouflaged behind glass block panes. I parked in a two-hour zone separated by a grass median from blue-and-whites and vans with steel-gridded windows, locked the .38 (and the contraband honorary Wayne County Sheriff's shield) in the glove compartment, and put myself through the same metal detectors you see everywhere these days, from Comerica Park to the Seventh Day Adventist Church.

A female turnkey with a sleeve patch modeled after the Michigan State flag looked at my driver's license and P.I. ticket, dropped them back into the steel tray, and chunked it out for me to retrieve them. From my side of the bulletproof Plexiglas she was an attractive brunette in her mid-thirties, her hair fixed behind her ears with barrettes and clear gloss on her nails.

"Who are you here to see?" Her tone was polite, pleasant, and burnished like chrome steel.

I'd left my name when I'd called, and of course it was right there on her metal clipboard, but I said, "Daniel Corbeil."

She nodded without checking the information against her list and directed me to the visitors' room.

I passed into a long narrow chamber brightly lit by LEDs through frosted panels in a suspended ceiling, where another turnkey—this one male, with a shaven head the color of toffee—instructed me to keep my voice at a normal conversational level, to make no physical contact with the inmate, and under no circumstances to pass anything to him without first submitting it for inspection. For all that, he came off as no firmer than a security guard in a suburban middle school. The really tough ones never feel the need to show it until push comes to shove; then it's a chokehold you'll still be feeling come Christmas.

A long laminated table divided the room, with no partition standing between resident and visitor; good lighting, stern training, and a rotation system in place to prevent routine boredom from leading to complacency made such restrictions superfluous. All of the warnings I'd been given were spelled out on signs mounted on the walls between the Bill of Rights and the smiling faces of the governor, the Michigan Secretary of State, and the members of the parole board. Cut-out construction-paper hearts pasted to the walls, signed by generous donors to the state corrections system, designed probably to soften the effect of enforced confinement, only contributed to the ghastly reality: Nobody from the entrance on the other side of the table was leaving the room except through that same door.

It wasn't much of a door, to look at. The steel core was faced with oak veneer, with a square window set into it, like the entrance from a doctor's reception area to the consulting rooms. Everything had been done to make the place seem like an ordinary professional building, from all appearances; there was even a unisex restroom for visitors. Somehow it made the whole experience seem all the more depressing. Too much money had been spent in order to preserve the clean cold efficiency of life on the outside, and too little to see to the comforts of those condemned to life on the inside. They were fed well, clothed adequately, hygiene and medical needs attended to, and sheltered from the worst of the history of incarceration; but it was all for show.

An inmate sat on the other side near the far end, across from a fat man in pinstripes with a glistening brown leather briefcase leaning against the leg of the table. They were speaking in tones too low to be heard from where I was, but evidently in what the guard considered a normal conversational level. He'd staked out his corner near the door from outside and stood at parade rest with his hands folded behind him.

I drew out a chair halfway down the table and sat down to wait and yearn for a cigarette. I wasn't sure just why I was there, apart from killing time until Alderdyce was available to furnish me with inside dope. Nothing Corbeil could tell me would add anything to the record; in fact, time could only have eroded what was fresh in the beginning, and artificially sweetened details grown stale, like eyewitness memories of the JFK assassination.

No, my reasons were entirely personal. The impression he made would be what I'd take away, either to go on from there or return his sister's check. Lawyers can afford to sweat for the guilty; I couldn't.

While I was waiting, the lawyerly type in pinstripes gathered up his briefcase and left and a guard buzzed himself in to return the inmate to his cell; nothing got past the surveillance camera mounted in a corner of the ceiling. The kind of quiet you don't find on the outside settled in.

The buzzer shattered it. A lock clunked and the door with the window in it opened. This uniform could have been the first one's twin, except he was three inches shorter and had a full head of hair, cut close and dyed dandelion yellow, Dennis Rodman fashion. He stood aside, holding the door for the man he'd escorted there from the cells.

Dan Corbeil was still recognizable from the photos taken of him in the late nineties, despite the sagging flesh of drastic weight loss, putty-colored jailhouse pallor, and a widow's peak that had thinned to a few colorless threads. His eyes were bright under boggy lids, but it was more the glitter of glass than alertness. That and the way he walked, sliding his feet on the waxed floor, and the aimlessness of his progress, coming up short against the chair on his side as if he hadn't seen the obstacle, painted a portrait of a man who'd abandoned all hope long before I came along.

I'd known it would be bad, but I hadn't guessed how bad. Springing an ostensibly innocent party from confinement is tough enough with authority stonewalling you at every turn; but you can usually draw strength from the party's cooperation. That wouldn't be the case this time. Where he was concerned, walls and bars and locks were only set-dressing. He was incarcerated in a penitentiary of his own mind.

I hoped to hell his sister was wrong about his innocence and I could return the advance and walk away from this one. If not, I'd be running a race against suicide.

SIX

Mr. Corbeil, my name is Amos Walker. I'm a private detective. Your sister hired me to investigate your case."

In the beginning I always call them by their last names, and never neglect the "Mr." Cops use first names, to establish intimacy, or what passes for it in the criminal justice system. Turnkeys who have watched too many old prison flicks snarl their last names only, or some bestial substitute to render them down to something less than human. It takes only a few extra syllables to create the illusion they're still part of civilized society; if only for the time it takes to pressure them.

The skinhead guard's stomach growled; that's how quiet the room got after I'd spoken. The inmate's eyes were empty. I gave up trying to meet them. When he parted his lips to respond, they made a noise like someone opening a Ziploc bag.

"My sister." It was a voice that had gone unused inside that airtight container for a week, dry and raspy. If he'd made friends inside, they were deaf-mutes.

"Young, blonde, about yea tall. Your parents named her after a posy."

That amused him—the way a breeze tickles a chain-link fence. "I know who she is. I can't get her to stop coming here."

"You can refuse to see her."

He shifted his weight in his chair. Said nothing.

"She's told me your version of what happened, or didn't. I'd like to hear it from you."

"Is that what she's paying you for? To get the same story over and over? Do you work for the government, Mr.—?"

I let that bait dangle. "It's like the telephone game; the more people pass on a piece of information, the more it gets twisted until it bears no resemblance to how it started out."

"Read the papers."

"I did. They practically invented the telephone game."

A spark glimmered in his eyes. It didn't stick long enough for the length of time it takes to describe it, but it hadn't shown before, even when he'd accused me of jacking up his sister for more money. That was supposed to be an expression of outrage, but it had come out stale, like telling someone to have a nice day.

But here was a foothold; a shallow one, not much more than a dimple. Compared to what he'd given me so far it was a grand staircase. Anyway I stuck my toe in it and tested it with my weight.

I said, "Just tell it like you're telling it for the first time. It's been long enough you might remember details you forgot when everything was still raw. I won't interrupt. The cops make a practice of that, just to trip you up."

He braced his hands on the table, started to push himself to his feet.

The sound I heard was my toehold crumbling. I couldn't even be sure if that spark had been genuine or I'd just wanted it to be there.

I got a little desperate. Every minute I kept him was another step closer to a goal that was so far away I might have been looking at it from the nosebleed section. "Okay, let's talk about something else. What do you like to read? Chrys says you studied architecture. I could bring you some books on that."

He smiled then; bitter and tight-lipped, as if he'd resealed the bag; but it was a change. "Anything you can find on this building, especially the drainage system."

"I didn't think the warden would okay showing *Shawshank* here."

"Guard."

Dennis Rodman had been hovering outside, watching through the window. Now he buzzed himself back in. Corbeil finished getting up. "You asked what I wanted. You can't deliver on that, how do you plan to get me out of here?"

I watched him leave with the turnkey.

I felt fine. It was an encouraging interview after all. If he could joke about escape, he hadn't given up entirely. Or even if it wasn't a joke. It didn't mean he was innocent—contrary to the popular view, very few convicts in this country are wrongfully accused, and most of their stories are plausible enough to raise doubts—but maybe it gave me room to maneuver. On the way home I stopped at the bank where everything had begun and cashed Chrys Corbeil's check. The cashier I got didn't know me from Barney Rubble. I'd had my fifteen minutes.

SEVEN

Of course he's innocent. They all are; just listen to 'em. It's our job to scare up men and women who have never committed an offense against society, and if we can't shoot them while they're in cuffs, we can at least load the dice in court. I'm on my third nightstick; ran out of space on the others for my notches."

It was another day, and it must have started all of a sudden for John Alderdyce. I'd tracked him down in the Second Precinct men's room. He'd sloughed off his suit coat, shirt, and tie, and bent before the long mirror above the sinks with a ribbed undershirt tucked into his pleated slacks, buzzing his shotgun stubble with a noise like a grinder plowing through iron grit. His heavy muscles didn't seem to have lost any definition, but the tattoo on his right biceps, of a grinning skull wearing a straw boater at a jaunty angle, had faded from deep blue to a washed-out turquoise. He'd had it done after a former police chief issued a ban on skin art. The chief had since served his time in Jackson over a pile of cash that fell out of his ceiling when his house was being remodeled, but John's tattoo was still there, if less vivid.

I said, "I can never tell when you're being serious or just joking."

"What do you want, Walker?"

"Whatever you've got on the April Goss murder. I read the papers. Now I want to know what happened."

"At the risk of derailing the fake-news express, I have to say this time they got it pretty much right." He stopped to blow whiskers out of his cordless razor and caught my eye in the mirror; he read my expression. "Yeah, I reviewed it. You didn't think I'd miss the connection between an eyewitness to bank robbery and a high-profile murder case, did you?"

"I toyed with the idea. That's your fault. During the week and a half you were retired the whole criminal justice system lost a couple of yards."

He slapped on aftershave lotion; something with a woodsy scent, probably hemlock spruce, heavy on the hemlock. "Do me a favor and keep that to yourself. Otherwise the chief will make a photo op out of me and I'll be back out on my can next time the administration changes hands. Pets are for home."

"So what's your take? Was the case locktight or looser than usual?"

"It had holes. If it didn't, I'd have ordered it reopened. Like a conspiracy theory, you know? All the pieces fit because someone put in overtime making 'em fit."

"As for instance."

"As for instance the autopsy report. It was sealed. The jury never got to hear that Goss wasn't pregnant after all."

"My client knew that. Someone must have unsealed it at some point."

"The point being it was after conviction. A go-getter with the *News* filed for it under the Freedom of Information Act. Not that it got him a byline, or even three inches in Section D, right next to the government contracts. By that time Corbeil was doing his second year in Jackson. He was old news, one hundred and fifty times removed by way of fresher homicides."

"Would it have made any difference if it had come out during his trial?"

"The defense might have tried to make the case that she'd found out she wasn't pregnant and told him; I suppose that might have occurred even to the glorified law clerk he drew in the p.d. lottery, but short of another pee stick or a record of a medical exam to confirm the possibility, the state's attorney would've brushed it aside without getting up off his ass. As far as anyone can prove, she died thinking she was in the family way. I don't think any attempt was made for a new trial based on the gag order."

"Why was the report sealed?"

Alderdyce hooked his shirt off the radiator and shook out the wrinkles. It was gunmetal-colored cotton with removable collar stays. "Ignorance may not be an excuse when you're in the dock, but it sure helps the incumbents when offices have changed hands. There'd been an election since the verdict came in. How much effort does it take to jerk your thumb over your shoulder and blame the guy that just left? And what's the guy who's no longer in the hot seat got to gain from a sudden attack of memory?"

"Take a wild guess."

"You should've asked me that back when I was a private citizen. Now I've got the weight of the System back on my shoulders. You know how tough it is prying anything out of us Establishment types."

"I would have asked back then—if I'd had a reason to know Dan Corbeil at the time."

I watched him adjust his silk necktie, taking the better part of a minute to eliminate the dimple, shrug his shoulders into his coat, smooth it down, and examine the effect in the mirror. His attention to his appearance wasn't effeminate, more a matter of military precision; he was a general preparing to review the troops. Without so much as issuing a memo, John Alderdyce had boosted most of the plainclothes division from TJ Maxx to Abercrombie & Fitch. Several chiefs had avoided being photographed next to him because he made their tailoring look like upholstery.

Notwithstanding all that, I said, "Anything else? Lip gloss? Glitter dust?"

He turned away from the mirror. You could never tell whether he was deep in thought or about to blow off the top of his skull; that Tiki god face never changed. "It's a mystery to me why you haven't raked in enough to open branch offices in all the major cities, the way you ask a favor from authority."

I hung a cigarette from my lip. It's against the law to set one afire in any public building in the state, but I needed to be doing something while I was waiting for the ocean to come to a boil.

"I can't help you," he said finally. "Maybe Chester Goss can; but he won't."

Chester Goss. That was worse than him losing his temper. I'd had the case two days and still I'd failed to make the connection: why April Goss's murder still resonated when so many more sensational crimes had dried up and blown away. Forget expanding my operation beyond Grand River Avenue; how I'd managed to keep even one office open was a mystery to me.

True to their name, Bloomfield, Bloomfield Hills, and Bloomfield Village had sprung up sometime past mid-century as suddenly as desert blossoms after a shower. As the money migrated north, the swank suburbs had swollen and split and multiplied, until today you need a certified mechanic to distinguish between the Corvettes and the Ferraris in the cobblestone driveways and tell you where the six-figure incomes end and the sevens begin. On the way I drove the Cutlass through an automatic car wash and popped for the deluxe scrub-and-wax. It didn't do anything for the dings, but in that area code, a mud wagon draws cops like fried cakes. I thought about asking the attendant for a receipt and charging it to expenses, but I figured Chrys Corbeil was still paying off her student loans, and anyway it was the first time I'd washed the heap since before Thanksgiving.

I steamed up Woodward shining like a tin trumpet, turned left onto Long Lake Road, once the site of Prohibition roadhouses and bobcat habitats, and slummed through a neighborhood of six-thousand-square-foot micromansions on the way toward the real currency. There, the contractors had salvaged old-growth oak from streams in Canada, imported monastery doors from Tuscany and the steppes of Russia, and numbered and dismantled stones from medieval Irish smokehouses for reassembly in backyards to store Jet Skis and snowmobiles.

Chester Goss lived in Pawnee Village, one of the newer tracts built during the brief hiatus between the end of white flight from Detroit and the return of the prodigals after the city came out of bankruptcy. It was virtually self-contained, with a Whole Foods market, high-end Italian and Mexican restaurants biting their thumbs at each other across a divided drive, a pocket-size movie theater, a boutique bookstore, and a gas station that sold everything from calamari embalmed in plastic to official Major League Baseball caps and, as long as you were there, gas. The HO-scale streets were christened after Native Americans and branched off into steadily diminishing estuaries, each bearing the same name as the original, only with a twist at the end: This was an effective ploy to confuse and discourage undesirable visitors.

I was more intrepid than that. I followed Geronimo Street to Geronimo Lane to Geronimo Court and finally entered Geronimo Circle, which like all the others had been resurfaced as recently as last week. It swept lagoon-fashion around an oval lot, where I steered into the curb in front of a low sprawling French country house built of native stone with a slate roof. Some clever architect had designed it to create the impression of a cozy cottage, an optical illusion to disguise the fact that it was the biggest house for blocks; it wouldn't fool the tax assessor, but might keep the neighbors from sneering over their cocktails about the unwashed new rich. A smaller oval next to the driveway contained an explosion of scarlet, indigo, magenta, and velvety white blooms that had been allowed to hang their heads casually over the whitewashed stone border in the style of an English garden. All the neighborhood architecture, in fact, seemed to fall into either the Gallic or Anglo-Saxon camp; in this case both. It appeared to be some sort of tribute to the French and Indian War.

The place whispered money. It had to whisper, given the circumstances. It was the house April Goss built.

At the time of his daughter's death, Chester Goss had worked as a regional assistant programming director for a group of premium TV channels owned by a corporation based in New Jersey. He'd publicly quit that job in order to devote his full time to investigating her reported murder on a local cable-access channel, turning up the heat on the criminal justice system five days a week. After Dan Corbeil's conviction he'd branched out to probe other unsolved crimes of violence. Six months later he was invited by a network to go coast-to-coast. As the show's talking head he publicized the cases, analyzed suspects, and racked up an impressive number of arrests and convictions with the help of tips supplied by viewers through his toll-free hotline. Fifteen years since it went national, *Cutthroat Dogs* had broken its own record for reality-programming viewership a half-dozen times. As I mounted the front porch, I wondered how he'd react to being on the receiving end of an interview.

EIGHT

It was an ordinary door—no ancient worm-eaten planks, no hand-forged iron hinges—just paneled oak, probably with a steel core. Ordinary, that is, except for the complete absence of a knob on the outside. No window or peephole either, but I followed the tingle in the back of my neck to a surveillance camera mounted above the frame. I used my thumb on a nacre button the size of a quarter. A dull gong thudded somewhere deep in the house.

"Who is it, please?"

A tense, reedy voice. I decided there was a speaker hidden behind the wrought-iron fretwork that decorated the wall on both sides of the door. The answer had come so quickly the owner had to have been standing near the mike when I rang.

"Amos Walker. I called earlier." I flipped open my folder and held it up to the camera next to my face.

"One moment."

It was a little longer than that while a number of snaps, clicks, clinks, and scrapes worked their way down from the top of the door to just below waist level. After that came a series of electronic beeps. I counted them. Not many alarm systems require ten digits to disarm.

The woman who opened it was almost as tall as I was, with broad square shoulders under a thin salmon-colored sweater buttoned at the neck and worn cape-fashion with her bare arms outside the sleeves. Vail Goss, Chester's wife, had aged twenty years since her picture had appeared in the papers at the time of the investigation into her daughter's death, but then she hadn't looked young under the stress of the period, so there wasn't much contrast. On the cusp of sixty, she was still what writers used to call a handsome woman. The lines in her face were barely skin-deep, her tight mouth wore a thin coat of orange, and her eyes were a smoky gray-green, the whites clear. Her jaw-length red hair looked natural. Each time she spoke, her high thin voice caught me by surprise. If someone pinched her she'd summon every dog in the neighborhood.

She pivoted away from the door—and from me. "Chet's in the den. Can I bring you a refreshment?"

I said no thanks and stepped into an entryway paved with green and white tiles. She used the hand not occupied resetting the locks to indicate a door standing open at the far side of the room. I didn't see her again after that.

As I approached the den, someone or something was grunting and panting inside. It sounded like a horse blowing after a hard gallop.

The room was small and octagonal, with a bump-out window beyond which more flowers drooped over a stone border. Framed community-service citations hung on the walls and a foot-high winged statuette on a pedestal hoisted a gilt globe on a small round table that seemed to have been designed to support it. A couple of easy chairs and a love seat, all upholstered in slate-blue squishy-looking leather, were pushed up against the walls, making room for the man jumping around in front of a forty-inch widescreen. His tennis whites were dark with sweat and he had a wicker basket shaped like a giant spoon strapped to his right forearm, which he used to smack a virtual ball toward an animated male figure on the screen. This character caught the ball on the bounce with an identical basket and returned fire.

I watched this for a while, my hands in my pockets. When it didn't look like he was going to turn around any time soon, I spoke.

"You realize if I couldn't see the TV, I'd think you were having some kind of seizure."

He didn't jump at the sound of my voice, although his back was to me and I'd raised it to be heard above the gasping and foot-thumping. With his free hand he scooped a cigar-shaped remote from a pocket of his shorts and flicked off the set and the DVD player using one button. He tossed it onto one of the shoved-back chairs, snatched a white towel off the arm, and mopped his face and the back of his neck. Then he turned to face me.

If *Hour Detroit* magazine could be trusted, Chester Goss was a few years older than his wife; he looked younger. Lean and tan, with vertically pleated cheeks and thinning dark hair cropped close, he looked like an advertisement for a prescription drug that promised you a life of hang-gliding, bike trips, and alligator wrestling despite your horrifying disease; when the drug companies sign a spokesman, they make sure he's of a certain age and in excellent health. This one had a wide, humorous mouth, but whatever joke it was enjoying was lost on his eyes. They were as flat and gray as lead slugs.

He unstrapped the gizmo from his arm, watching me the whole time. "Jai alai. My PR guy talked me into taking a commercial DNA test, to reel in a sponsor. Turns out I'm Basque on my mother's side. I'd thought I was as English as Gladstone's pup. Naturally it led to an Iberian binge; I learned Spanish *and* Basque, vacationed in Madrid, ate bull's testicles straight from the arena. This is the only thing that stuck. It's brutal, even if you're only competing against a cartoon. My face is too well-known to play a real game in the real world without interruption. Mr. Walker?"

"Guilty."

He looked at a sports watch strapped to his left wrist. "Right on time. You must know how important that is to a former television programmer."

I nodded. "Same time, same station."

Goss slung the towel around his neck, flung the basket—I suppose it's called a racquet—into a chair, and closed the distance to shake my hand. His grip was what you'd expect of someone who hops about batting around pretend balls with a simulated opponent. When he let go I flexed blood back into my fingers and pointed one at the gold statuette on the round table. "That's the first Emmy I've seen outside a TV screen."

"Prime-time reality. I was up against *American Ninja* and the umpteenth reboot of *Big Brother*. Could've been worse. I started out in daytime. That would have put me in the category with Jerry Springer."

"And you thought jai alai was brutal."

He had a square smile. His teeth were perfect. What other kind of work he'd had done was strictly between himself and his specialists.

I asked him how *Cutthroat Dogs* was doing.

"I never check. If the ratings are good I don't need to know it, and if they're bad I don't want to remind my sponsors they're backing a dodo. I just signed on for three more seasons, so I guess it's holding its head above water. The number of dangerous felons who have been apprehended based on tips from my viewers is a more accurate barometer of the show's success. We just cracked a thousand."

"Congratulations."

"Congratulations to us all." He used a corner of the towel to dab perspiration from behind one ear. "You know, my earliest sponsor insisted I call it *Monsters Among Us*; dropped me when I refused. That's what they are, wild animals that prey on the weak. I was a year getting cable access under my title. I'm not sure whether the yellow-bellies were afraid of offending dog-lovers or cutthroats. Anyway, by the time the networks signed on, a dozen wannabes had sprung up with some version of the same thing. A successful title is the title of a successful show.

"Anyway, that's what the boobs who run the tube think. As they see it, it's always the public's fault when the ratings don't deliver; but it's always the show that gets the axe."

He excused himself to take a shower and told me to make myself at home. While he was gone I took the tour. He'd been commended by police and sheriff's departments throughout Southeastern Michigan, two governors, the Detroit Police Officers Association, and the Michigan Bar. There was a framed photograph of him sitting in an easy chair opposite Mike Wallace; I remembered Goss had been one of his last interviews on *60 Minutes.*

There was something missing, but I didn't know whether to bring that up.

A distant whirring of water stopped with a clunk and he came back a few minutes later, wearing a pale yellow sports shirt outside gray slacks with a knife-edge crease, tasseled loafers on his feet. His face was ruddy and he'd slapped on something that smelled like sunned leather.

"You said on the phone you're looking into April's murder." He tipped a hand toward a sling chair. I took it and he took the one opposite and crossed his legs.

"I'm hoping to clear up that sealed-evidence business."

"May I ask who you're representing?"

"That's confidential."

The corners of that humorous mouth turned upward a millimeter, spreading the pleats in his face. "I can guess: Some do-gooder out to reform our justice system, trying to reopen cases that were closed to everyone's satisfaction years ago."

"Something like that," I said. "I don't know about the do-gooder part, and I've never known everyone to be satisfied, ever."

"My station gets letters and e-mails after every broadcast. The whole shop's broken, they say, and what we need to do is raze it and rebuild it from the ground up. Better to let a hundred guilty men go free than to imprison one honest one."

"That *is* the system."

"Bullshit. I'd stake this house on the certainty that not one of those bleeding hearts lost a close relative to some cutthroat dog."

His voice remained steady, but a flint sparked in his eyes. I moved a shoulder. "I don't own anything I could stake against it. I wondered if you had any idea why the fact that your daughter wasn't pregnant was withheld from the jury that convicted Daniel Corbeil."

"Does it matter? They were out less than three hours and there wasn't a single holdout all through the deliberations."

"My client wants to know whether that would still be true if the defense could have used the evidence to cast doubt on motive."

"Possibly not. But they all would have come around eventually. You should have seen their faces during summations. You could have cracked walnuts on eight of them."

"You haven't answered my question, Mr. Goss."

"No. I have no idea why the decision was made. You'd have to ask the judge, but that would be difficult because he's been dead for years. I suppose you could file a motion to unseal all the records; but that would take time and involve court costs your client can't cover. Huron Valley doesn't exactly pay its inmates minimum wage. You *are* representing Corbeil, aren't you?"

I wasn't, but if I told him I wasn't, he'd jump to the next conclusion, this time the right one. Chrys Corbeil had already had her portion of what the media could do to a private citizen.

"Mr. Goss, can you tell me why there are no photos of your daughter in this room?"

He uncrossed his legs and stood up. "That's it. Leave."

I felt my eyebrows touch my hairline. "It was a—"

"I know what it was. You think I've stopped caring. I don't need to decorate my home with reminders to keep the pain alive. Some days I wake up, full of relief that I had a ghastly dream. Then I remember, and it's that first horrible day all over again fresh."

"I didn't—"

"If you're not out of this house in two minutes I'll file a restraining order against you. I may file it anyway."

Still I kept my seat. "No judge would comply. I haven't said or done anything that could be interpreted as a threat."

"Don't be so sure. Get out."

Vail Goss was nowhere in sight, leaving me to undo all the locks and latches to let myself out. I didn't mind. I had what I'd come for: The name of the man responsible for the seal.

NINE

My stomach was scraping my spine. In Southfield I pulled into a strip mall and ordered a steak sandwich and a martini in a sports bar next door to a pet-groomer's. On the TV monitors a couple of ex-jocks in loud blazers were conducting a post-mortem on last night's Pistons match. My waitress was a blonde with no-nonsense eyes who would always be forty. She got everything right, including how I liked my steak and the gin-vermouth ratio. I told her. She glanced down at my tip.

"Next time ask for Claire. Your station's my station."

Barry Stackpole was sitting behind the desk in my office with his ankles crossed on the top. One of them was made of graphite. I remembered when it was hickory. He'd come back from the slaughter in Cambodia with all his pieces intact, only to lose some of them to a TNT charge wired to the ignition of his Buick Skylark. Back then he'd specialized in covering the mob, which didn't approve.

Now he studied truly hazardous issues: international terrorism, human trafficking, and local politics.

He tossed aside the Obama-era newsmagazine he'd taken from my waiting room. "Can't remember when I was here last. Nothing's changed, including the dead flies on the sill."

"I change them out now and then. My super owes me an apology. He guaranteed the dead bolt."

"It's not the lock. Your door's got erectile dysfunction; sagged just enough the bolt won't make contact with the socket. I slipped the spring latch with my Medicare card."

He didn't look as if he was eligible. His tanned features, thick fair hair, and athletic build had stopped deteriorating years before that magazine hit the racks. Apart from some laugh lines around his pale eyes, he could've passed for my baby brother. We were the same age.

I made myself uncomfortable in the customers' chair. "What brings you to the Million-Dollar Mile?"

"Curiosity, what else? Did Corbeil do it?"

"You and Alderdyce. It doesn't take Stephen Hawking to connect my teller to the April Goss case, but you both act like the canary that swallowed the cat. What do *you* think? You've had time to bone up."

"I'm not Perry Mason. I couldn't care less who's innocent. I feed on the guilty." He waggled the hand missing two fingers. "For what it's worth, I never was satisfied with how it came out."

"The pregnancy test cover-up?"

"Before that. That media blitz Goss engineered made me ashamed for my profession. Defendants are supposed to be tried in court, not between a Faygo ad and the weather; says so somewhere in the National Archives."

"That doesn't make him innocent."

"It makes you want him to be. Who'd you talk to, apart from the off-and-on police inspector?"

"Who would I?"

"Goss and Corbeil."

"Other way around."

"Raise anything?"

I shook out a cigarette, but paused before lighting it. "Who am I talking to, Barry, you or your earbuds?"

"Look who's gone publicity shy. Just the other day you begged me for as much as you could get."

"I was younger then, and naïve."

Same hand, different gesture. I took that to mean we were off the grid. "A fistful of hunch," I said. "Corbeil's hanging on by his eyelashes; could blink any time. I'm pretty sure it was Goss threw the wraps over the pregnancy results."

"Big ratings are no shield from an indictment for evidence-tampering."

"I said it was a hunch. The judge who signed off on the deal is dead. I'd never get a court order to look at the file for action, and even if I did, get whoever put it in motion to admit it and what he got for it."

"You sure won't if you don't try. Let me rattle a few cages."

I lit up and squinted through the smoke. "Literally?"

"You know how many lawyers have batted in the exercise yard for mixing up the letter and the spirit of the law?"

"What's the tariff, a case of Jack or an exclusive?"

"Can't a friend do a favor for a friend?"

I grinned. "'Someday, and that day may never come . . .'"

"I said 'favor,' Don Vito. I didn't say I'd come to you with a ca-daver." He put his feet on the floor and stood. "You and I go back, Amos. That means something."

I wanted to agree; but genuine sentiment wasn't in Barry's tackle box. Like he said, he and I went back.

He was barely gone when someone triggered the buzzer in the waiting room. Without that, I might not have heard the knock on the door marked PRIVATE. It sounded like a woodpecker with a headache. I called out an invitation.

Vail Goss took her fashion tips from the 1952 Sears & Roebuck catalogue. She wore a moss-green tweed suit tailored to her trim waist and square shoulders, low heels, a gray felt hat bent into an inverted U, and white cotton gloves. The hat was trimmed with a black veil that barely reached to her hairline. I couldn't see the point.

I rose. Given her general appearance I didn't feel self-conscious doing it. I asked her to sit.

She closed the door without making any noise and perched on the edge of the chair with her knees together and rested her hands on the clutch purse in her lap. She'd put something on her face that masked the few lines it wore, but although the suit and hat brought out the smoky hazel in her eyes, they looked old and tired and sick.

"I came to apologize for the way my husband acted. He's really not in the habit of throwing visitors out of the house."

"He's pretty good at it for someone who doesn't practice." I sat.

"You don't know what he has to put up with all the time. People seldom write to TV stations because they're pleased with what they saw, and now that most of them do it by e-mail, they've lost all semblance of decency. The language they use! And it's always the ones who claim they're offended by something he said on the air."

"I'm not offended, Mrs. Goss. Neither is my client. We're just trying to get at the truth. If that means Dan Corbeil belongs in prison, I've done my job. Your husband is a journalist. He doesn't need anyone to explain that."

"He doesn't; but there's a difference between objective reporting and what happened to—to our April." Her breath caught in her throat.

"Would you like a drink of water?" It was lame.

"I don't suppose you have anything stronger."

That made me feel less idiotic. I swiveled to the safe, broke out a bottle of Cutty, and held it up. She nodded, her face brightening a little. I grabbed two Old Fashioneds and got up to use the tap in the water closet.

She guessed what I had in mind. "Neat, please."

It didn't go with her outfit. She should have asked for something tall and green with a garden in it. I poured two inches into each glass and slid one across to her.

She dipped her upper lip in the Scotch and smacked it against the lower; she was drinking not just because she needed it, but also because she enjoyed it. I hoped I wasn't going to start liking her. It would interfere with the clean metallic workings of my ice-cold brain.

"Does your husband know you're here, Mrs. Goss?"

"He'd be furious. I told him I was going to Somerset Mall. I will, after I leave. I need some things and I don't like to lie." She took another sip and smiled nervously. "This is the first time I've been to Detroit in years."

"It's not so bad, if you know which parts to stay away from."

"I suppose you do."

"They're where I work. You didn't have to come all the way down here to apologize for Chester. You could have phoned."

She drank another quarter-inch and leaned forward to set the glass on the desk; just enough out of her reach to avoid going for it automatically. When she sat back, she looked more relaxed, or at least less like she was going to jump up and dart into a hole like a chipmunk.

I took my first drink and sat back myself, rolling the glass between my palms. "Why are you really here?"

"You implied Daniel Corbeil is innocent. Is he?"

"Only he knows the answer to that. It's unlikely, statistically speaking. Our system's pretty sound."

"Then, why—?"

"I said *pretty* sound. 'Beyond reasonable doubt' leaves a hole big enough for some people to fall through."

"I must warn you, if you manage to free that young man, you'll make a powerful enemy in Chet."

"It shouldn't have to be that way. If it turns out Corbeil *is* innocent, it means whoever killed your daughter and rigged it to look like suicide is still out there."

That made stretching her arm to retrieve her drink worth the effort. It brought dawn to her cheeks. "I hadn't really thought of it that way. I guess it's a no-brainer; but, you see, I've spent twenty years certain the man who did that ghastly thing is paying for it."

"It's not my job to convince you. It's not even my job to spring him, only to go over all the columns and make sure they add up. If they don't and he walks, it won't be because of a technicality. It'll be because he's spent twenty years paying somebody else's bill. Do you know if Chester's the one who got the evidence your daughter wasn't pregnant quashed at the trial?"

"No." But she said it quickly enough it was clear the question came as no surprise.

"No, he didn't, or no, you don't know?"

"Both."

I shook my head. "It can't be both. If you know he didn't, you can't not know, and if you don't know, you can't say he didn't. See how it works?"

"Now you sound like that defense attorney in court, trying to trip up the witnesses against Corbeil."

"Which is it, Mrs. Goss?"

"No. I *don't* know. But if he did, can you blame him? You said innocent people don't go to jail often, but I'm sure you'll agree that the guilty go free all the time. Sometimes the system needs a little help."

I said nothing.

She set her glass back in the wet circle it had made on the desk. It already had more rings than the Olympics flag. "If Corbeil didn't kill April, and if whoever did is still around, will you set out to find that person?"

"If someone hires me to."

"Someone will." She stood, holding her purse in front of her like a shield. "Thank you for seeing me. Somehow I trust you."

"Thank you for that." I got to my feet and accepted the hand she offered. Her grip was as firm as Goss's.

A cloud passed across her face. "You won't—"

"Not a word."

After she left I finished my drink, dumped hers out into the water closet sink, and rinsed the glasses. The buzzer came again as I was shutting the safe. Chrys Corbeil came in, bringing with her a fresh breeze of youth. Today it was business wear, a white nylon blouse with a tan jacket, a blue scarf around her neck, black slacks with a crease, and sandals, no purse. She'd swept her pale blond hair behind her ears, which accentuated the diamond shape of her face.

"Back at work?" I said when we were both seated.

"Tomorrow. I'm acclimating." Her eyes asked the question she'd carried in.

I said, "Nothing I'd take to your bank, but it's early days. I've barely dented your retainer."

"Keep it, please. I've decided not to go ahead with the investigation."

"Uh-huh."

"You don't seem surprised."

"There comes a moment on almost every job when the client wants to call it off. Sometimes I let them, but they have to make the case first."

"I went to see Dan this morning."

"Did he bawl you out for hiring me?"

"Yes! I've never seen him so angry. He asked me what right I had to stick my nose into his problem; he shouted it, over and over. The guard had to pull him out of the visitors' room. He was afraid Dan would attack me physically."

"Good."

"Not good. He'd never lay a hand on me or anyone else. That's what I hired you to prove, but it's not worth it if it makes him more miserable than he already was. Mr. Walker, I'm terribly afraid he'll do something to himself."

"He won't. That's why I said 'good.' I wasn't talking about what the guard did. I was talking about your brother no longer being a zombie. If he can raise enough of a mad to scream at you, it means he's got the bottom to stick it out till we've got an answer, one way or the other."

She shook her head violently enough to swing her hair out from behind her ears. "How could you know that? You're not a psychiatrist."

"Yesterday, when I offered to bring him some reading material, he made a joke about escape. If he can talk about that, and even poke fun at it, he isn't beyond help. I was sure of it then and I'm even more sure of it now. This isn't my first job. It's not even the first time I've represented the interests of a convict. I've been behind bars myself; not hard time, but with no clear idea of when or if I'd get out, which is just as bad if not worse. When are you going back?"

"Not until the weekend. The bank's already given me more time than I should have taken. I can't count on the vice president's goodwill forever."

"Make you a deal. Let me work this until your next visit. If neither one of you has changed your mind, I'll step off, and you won't owe me a cent."

She agreed.

I placed a few calls, made some appointments for tomorrow, and clocked out. A slab-sided midnight-blue sedan sat in front of my house, its twin pipes smoking thickly in the chill air of evening. The windows were tinted too dark for state law. That and the bilious green glow of its onboard computer made it a police vehicle. As I slowed to swing into my driveway, the driver's door opened and Detective First-Grade Stan Kopernick got out. I wondered what had taken him so long.

TEN

"So this is where you slip into your mules, sip your orange pekoe," he said, tilting his big head toward the house. "Looks like where Hansel and Gretel'd hang out if they were Polacks."

The place stands across the street from the city of Hamtramck, founded by Polish immigrants, but now as polyethnic as the rest of metropolitan Detroit. Even a guy named Kopernick could say *Polack* and still sound racist.

"I got rid of the gingerbread years ago. Ants." I held my keys with my hand looped through the oversize ring. Old habit; I hadn't had to use knucks in years.

He showed his lower teeth in a shark's grin. The man was as changeless as the Pictured Rocks: the heavy handsome face under the wool-felt hat, black brows, prominent but not beaky nose, wide mouth, roomy camel's-hair coat over pinstripes and matching burgundy shirt-and-necktie set, the way they sell them in boxes in the men's department, Florsheims on his feet.

As usual it was the facial scar that caught my attention first, a tiny white crescent just right of the cleft in the blue chin. If he'd been hit just a little harder I could have identified the signet in the ring that made it. Which might have been hard enough to prevent whatever he'd done in response.

A crack had opened in the timetables of history, just wide enough for Detective First-Grade Stanley Kopernick to fall through into our century directly from the 1940s. No other rational explanation suggested itself.

"Well, we gonna stand out here basking in the spring weather or step inside and shake the icicles off our dicks?"

"Since you put it that way," I said, shaking loose the key to the front door.

I snapped on the floor lamp in the living room, illuminating the tired furniture, the mild clutter, and the bits of decoration that had been in place so long I'd stopped seeing them. At least he had the grace—or whatever passed for it in him—not to comment.

"If you're one of those cops who never drink on duty, you can watch me." I headed for the kitchen.

He followed me. "My old man told me never to refuse free liquor. I loved my old man."

From the cabinet above the sink I hoisted down the economy-size jug of Old Smuggler and filled two of those glasses that come free with good Scotch at Christmas. It wasn't good Scotch.

This time he hadn't the grace. "Save the toney stuff for the gentry, I guess."

"I keep the high octane at the office. Get drunk at home."

He fisted his glass and put the top half down his throat. "Boozing over the sink's for the help."

"Get that from the old man?"

"No, I come to it myself. He *was* the help."

I let him have the only comfortable chair in the living room. He'd have taken it anyway. I found the sweet spot in the love seat, between the Bermuda Triangle in the center and the spring coiled to strike at the east end.

"This is cozy." He shucked off his coat sitting, letting it drape itself over the back of the chair, and crossed his legs, resting his glass on his knee. A sliver of shin as white and hairless as a fluorescent tube showed above his socks. "Like a guy and his old man grabbing a beer on the corner."

"Drop the hammer, Kopernick. I may be old enough to be your old man, but we both know you came from a spore."

He wet his upper lip in his drink and flicked it dry with a thumb. "Scuttlebutt is you're mucking around in the tar pits, looking for moldy old bones."

"I like moldy old bones. It's the bloody ones get me in trouble with cops. You'll have to be more specific, Detective. You wear subtle like a rat in a raincoat."

That one stung. Streaks of red came to the tops of his cheeks. That first gulp of Scotch hadn't brought so much as pale pink. Go figure. "I'm a guest in your house," he said. "You call me vermin?"

"I had to try. That spore dig got me zilch."

"I don't like rats. My first assignment when I was in the blue bag was bodyguarding Pest Control after a couple of 'em got shot at while trying to trap the buggers in vacant lots. One of the little bastards tried to run up my pants leg. I shot it off the toe of my shoe. Took a chunk off my best Thom McAn."

I lifted my glass to my lips, watching him over the rim. His color faded. Sitting there with his legs crossed, he looked comfortable and sleepy. So does a crocodile just before it lunges.

"I won't pump you for your client's name," he said. "I know how far that'd get me, and I got a good idea who it is. That was some deal you pulled off in the bank. I don't guess she said thanks with just a fruit basket."

That one whiffed past without me swinging at it. I said, "I was lucky. No oil tankers sank that day, and Congress was out; it was just me and Hägar the Horrible. I've heard from everyone but the Pope."

"It was me, I'd of aimed higher. My old turnout sarge would of booted me from here to Flint if I shot just to wound. That was before they made us swap our heavy artillery for cap guns, to give the maggots a chance."

"I had the same training. But you're not here to compare vermin."

He tugged his lower lip back up over his teeth. I relaxed a little then. When he got serious he was almost affable. Almost everything about him was opposite to everyone else I'd known. "You know I worked the April Goss case."

"Hard not to. There weren't any tankers going down then either."

"Yeah. You might say it's what made me. I happened to wander in front of a camera first day of a deal that just kept on playing and playing. You can bust your ass every day for years, keep your nose clean as morning dew, and never draw a glance from the top if you don't catch a break like that."

"It's Detroit," I said. "Not Santa's workshop."

"You're telling me." He tossed off the rest of his drink, leaned forward and thumped the glass down on the coffee table. He stayed in that position, elbows resting on his knees with his hands dangling between them, his face close enough to mine to smell the heather on his breath. "You're expecting the layoff speech, but I'm gonna surprise you. How'd you like a little help from the department?"

I played for time. I didn't care for what was happening. Once a predator goes against nature, you can never see *Animal Planet* the same way.

"Maybe I was wrong about Santa."

"That a yes or a no?"

"It's a give me a minute while I count my fingers."

"You don't trust me. I got over that a long time ago." He drywashed his palms. They made a sound like someone sanding a floor. "Things are getting stale: Shootings on the west side, domestic beefs downriver, junkies making off with tip cups from Starbucks. Same shit every day, only different people. You can't make sergeant on that. This bird Corbeil's guilty as O. J.; you know it, I know it—hell, little sis knows it, she just hopes to stir up enough dust to get him a ride down to County for the scenery change. CONVICTED MURDERER GETS SECOND CHANCE: The press'll eat it up, they're as bored as I am counting bullet holes. This town hasn't seen a good legal drama since we put away the mayor."

"Meaning you get to step back up to the plate."

"I got the suit all picked out," he said. "Charcoal gray, amethyst stripes: conservative but smart. Last time I gave testimony in this case was in the old blue bag. So what's the verdict?"

"I'll take it under advisement."

He made a new face. "I wish just once when a guy gets the blow-off somebody'd tell him he's getting the blow-off. I'd buy that guy a box at Comerica Park."

"To tell you the truth, I'm still processing 'amethyst.'"

He showed his teeth again. "I flipped through *GQ* in Supercuts. They didn't have any *Guts 'n' Glory*."

"Thanks for dropping by, Detective. I don't get the chance to entertain very often."

"I don't doubt it, the liquor you stock." Big and solid as he was, he slid from that deep chair and into his coat all in one smooth oiled motion.

After he left I picked up the phone, then put it back down. I got up and opened the front door in time to see him start his engine and swing into the street. A man with his unlikely grace was capable of creeping back up the front steps without making a sound and eavesdropping through the keyhole; in this game a little paranoia is as useful as a lot of curiosity.

On the way back through the living room I picked up my glass with the idea of freshening my drink, but changed my mind when I got to the sink and dumped what was left of it down the drain. I could feel that steak sandwich wallowing in the puddle in my stomach. I rinsed out the glass, filled it with tap water, washed the taste of Old Smuggler out of my mouth, and went back to the telephone.

"Miss me already?" Barry sounded bright as Christmas morning. I decided he really had given up drinking.

"Guess who dropped in for tea?"

"Since you sound like a record winding down, I'd say it's a cop."

"Not just any cop." I told him about Kopernick.

"Man, when you go fishing for clients you ought to stick to fresh water. Those bottom-feeders don't make good eating."

"I'm thinking of doing all my banking from home from now on. That's what got me into this mess."

"How'd he put it? I'm guessing out in the open. Kopernick's idea of a veiled threat is to tell you your shoe's untied and knee you in the face when you bend down."

"He offered me the use of the department."

I heard a long low whistle on his end. It could have been the connection. "Any signs of a stroke?"

"His kind doesn't have strokes. They give 'em. He *says* he wants another turn at bat on the Goss case. Not getting enough love from the chief."

"Horseshit. He wants to install a cookie in your hard drive. That means—"

"I know what it means. I saw it in *Wired* at Supercuts. They were out of *Horse 'n' Buggy*. I'm tempted to take him up on it."

"You're right. He does give people strokes."

"Not this time. I can bake cookies too."

"Oh. Risky. Did you call me to come looking for you when you disappear?"

"I called you to find out what kind of jam he's in."

ELEVEN

Ambient air stirred on Barry's end. After a moment: "Pleasant as that is to contemplate, it could be what he said. Once you've been in the spotlight you miss the heat."

"Just the fact my job exists acts on him like a flesh-eating virus. If it's all about making a splash with the chief, he'd find a way to do it without busting an ulcer."

"The minute I start asking around, Kopernick will know it," he said. "Sure you know what you're doing?"

"Practically never. But the client's feet are getting cold, and I've got to pull an ace out of my sleeve before she jumps ship. Or in any case a card that will pass for one."

"That hard up?"

"No more than always. This case is starting to turn. If I don't follow it through I may never get the stink out of my nose."

I heard him shaking his head twenty-six blocks uptown. "I used to wonder why a guy like you would stick in such a rotten line of work. That was before mine took the turn it did."

"Poor baby."

"Fuck you."

I went to bed.

———

Over coffee and what passed for breakfast I thumbed through the notes I'd taken in the library downtown. The name of the young public defender who'd stood up for Dan Corbeil was Michael Mihalich. I craned up the metropolitan directory and ran a crust of toast down the columns under ATTORNEYS and found a smiling middle-aged face in a quarter-page display ad for M. C. Mihalich in Eastpointe, specializing in disability cases. On his end of the line a minty cool female voice repeated my name and offered to set me up with an appointment next week.

"Actually I was hoping to see him today."

"I'm afraid that—"

"Tell him it's about the Corbeil case."

That meant as much to her as the capital of Belarus. From the timbre of her voice she was playing Easy-Bake Oven with her girlfriends when that one went down.

"What is your business, Mr."—pause to retrieve the name, I didn't think—"Walker?"

"Detective."

That got about as much reaction as expected. These days everyone's had enough business with the criminal justice system not to scamper up any walls when they come into its orbit. She asked me to please hold and played me sixteen bars of Air Supply. Already I didn't like M. C. Mihalich.

A man came on the line in mid-whimper. "This is Michael Mihalich. What department are you with?"

"No department. I'm a private investigator representing a client."

"Daniel Corbeil?"

I hadn't anything to lose by showing my cards. It was the nature of this beast that almost everyone I made contact with guessed the truth. "His sister."

He was silent a tick. "I guess she'd be grown up now."

"You were the lawyer who defended him during his trial?"

"If you can call it that. I didn't have much to work with."

"That's what I want to talk with you about."

"I can't discuss this over the phone."

I grinned at the window looking out on my neighbor's cedar fence. "Mr. Mihalich, I was just about to say the same thing."

Eastpointe had spent most of its history as East Detroit, in spite of the fact that it lies north of the city the residents don't want any part of; maps are strictly for pirates and world explorers. Changing the name of the suburb didn't make the situation any clearer. It's west of Grosse Pointe, Grosse Pointe Woods, and Grosse Pointe Farms, all places ritzier than a community struggling just to stay in the middle class.

It was a long straight sweep at a forty-five-degree angle up Gratiot, an avenue that might have been drawn by an architect using a steel rule, and probably was. The local transportation authority, after it got around to scrapping the mainframe computer that had been directing traffic locally since Nixon, finally got the timing down; if you started out on the right beat, it turned the lights green all the way. I glided past a dizzy succession of side streets lined with cozy-looking houses with sleeping flower gardens, followed blocks of automobile dealerships, car washes, and party stores, and swung right on Nine Mile Road. There the old downtown stood preserved in jars containing free-standing extinct hardware stores with fading Coca-Cola signs painted on the brick, and inside them antique furniture in rented booths. Past them and along a string of one-story mini-malls, flat-roofed and sheltering shops linked by common walls.

M. C. Mihalich Legal Services was in one of these. I knew the general address; the building had housed an H&R Block, and before that a Hallmark, and a pharmacy before that. From the look of it, before long it would host a dollar store, as likely as not in Mihalich's place. There was nothing shabby about the setup. The brickwork was good, the big front windows sparkling, the infrastructure probably sound, but it had the impersonality of one of those places that swept businesses in and out like blown leaves.

The establishment was a far cry from *L.A. Law.* A copper bell mounted on a spring clip above the door tinkled when I pushed it open, and a slim receptionist of nineteen or so looked up at me from behind a desk eight feet in. Her black hair was cut short and clung to her long skull like a polished onyx bowl. From the waist up she was dressed professionally, in an autumn-orange blazer over a plain black top, but the desk was transparent Lucite, showing a pair of brown legs in white shorts, flip-flops on her bare feet. Her fingers hovered above the keyboard of a laptop computer.

"Amos Walker," I said. "I think we spoke earlier."

"Oh, yes. I'll tell him you're here." Her crisp cool tone confirmed it. She pressed a key on a flat intercom and did that. I didn't hear his response, but I guessed what it would be.

"He'll be with you in a few moments, Mr. Walker. Please have a seat."

A row of connected seats faced the desk and beyond it a door with PRIVATE fixed to the printed woodgrain in stick-on gold letters. The seats were made of black Naugahyde stretched over hollow aluminum and might have come that way the last time they remodeled Metro Airport. I took one and wanted a cigarette while I browsed the wall art, daubs of color I'd seen in Pier One, in the same glass frames. Mihalich, on his side of the wall, would be rearranging things on his desk or sharpening pencils or learning to yodel. Disability cases are handled by boilerplate correspondence and are rarely urgent.

His practice wasn't lively in any event. In the ten minutes I spent recrossing my legs the telephone didn't ring once.

When the big moment came the brunette got off the speaker and said Mr. Mihalich would see me.

He was courteous, rising from behind a sleek oval of imitation black walnut and reaching out a hand that had a reasonable amount of resistance in its grip. He looked like his smiling picture in the directory: shaved head, long eager face without a wrinkle, eyebrows so pale they looked shaven too, so that he appeared permanently surprised and delighted to greet you. He had on a gray-and-black small-check sport coat, an open-neck shirt without a tie, and tan Dockers; never a wise choice when you're packing a spare tire. The mesh belt made a hammock for his belly. He looked younger than he was, but at my age you see youth everywhere.

"I was half expecting a hat and a trench coat," he said.

"No, you weren't. Even disability attorneys meet their share of private investigators."

The humorous expression slipped just a notch. "It was meant to break the ice; but I see you have your own formula."

I followed his open palm into a varnished plywood chair on my side of the desk, an Eames knockoff that was almost as uncomfortable as the real thing. There was a photo cube on the desk. The two sides I could see contained a pretty strawberry blonde in a printed sundress squinting against the sunlight and a little boy with a bulbous forehead and jaw and a sweet expression. That sponged the bad taste out of my mouth that had been left by his choice of music. I'm a bucket of mush.

"Nice little family," I said.

Mihalich sat on a swivel that sighed pneumatically under his weight. "My wife's a school nurse, which comes in handy. The boy has Down syndrome." He slung an arm over the back of his chair. "How is Corbeil? I assume you interviewed him."

"In prison. How do you think?"

He didn't blink. "If you're trying to make me feel guilty he's there, it's no go. I gave him as good a defense as anyone could, two years out of law school."

"I'm not trying to make you feel guilty. That word gets batted around too much, like 'starving' and 'killing.' It takes on a different meaning when it comes from twelve jurors and you're sitting in the hot seat. Anyway, when you're forced to skate with a blindfold on, you can't be expected to pull off a triple Axel."

"What blindfold is that, Mr. Walker?"

"Would it have made any difference if you were able to introduce the results of April Goss's autopsy during the trial?"

"They were introduced. The prosecution introduced them. I couldn't shake the medical examiner during the cross from his conviction that she didn't take her own life."

"I didn't mean that, the blood work, last meal eaten, progress of digestion. You'd have to look in a fallout shelter for a juror who isn't familiar with all that from *Law and Order* and *Police Academy Three*. I mean the pregnancy examination."

He'd rested one of his palms on the glossy desktop. There wasn't a wet patch there when he lifted it in a gesture that didn't mean anything. "After all this time, I couldn't say. I do know that the entire experience persuaded me not to go into criminal law."

"Pension cases can be just as dirty. Fly-by-night trucking companies will spend a couple of thousand to avoid paying out five hundred in benefits."

"You don't know the half of it. But I've been at it long enough to spot all the angles, and on the rare occasion I miss one, it doesn't involve locking up an innocent man for life."

"So you think Corbeil's innocent."

Mihalich sat back, releasing a fresh gasp from his chair. His smile was thin as electroplate. That, and his general deportment, told me all I wanted to know. This wasn't the same green lawyer who'd represented Dan Corbeil.

"I didn't say that," he said. "I can't tell you if I ever thought he was: Honestly. Some people are cut out to try such cases, go home, crack open a beer, and watch the Pistons lose without another thought to the day, just as some people can work in a pet shelter and get so used to it they don't smell the cyanide gas anymore. And that's good, because they're no use to anyone if they can't separate themselves from the action and do the job with a clear head. A sentimental slob like me would be the worst thing that could happen to a client fighting for his freedom. I would do it if I could, but I can't, so I don't."

"Okay."

"Okay?"

"Okay, because what happened twenty years ago isn't what I came here to ask."

TWELVE

The shallow clicking of the receptionist tapping keys outside drifted into the office; it was that quiet.

"I can't do that," Mihalich said finally. "This isn't door-to-door sales. I can't just approach someone cold and ask him to retain me as his attorney. It's unethical."

"No, just tacky. Ambulance chasers do it all the time."

His look of perennial surprise became something else. "For someone who's asking for an impossible favor, you sure suck at choosing vocabulary."

"I've been told that more recently than you'd think," I said. "If I'm rude, it's because I haven't got the time to brush up on my Emily Post. If I don't have something to show my client by this weekend, I won't have a client."

"What makes you think he'd want anything to do with me after the way his trial turned out?"

"You know the answer to that better than I would. Your work involves turning people's attitudes around to match yours."

His chair wheezed as he leaned forward and rested his forearms on the desk. "Are you retaining my services?"

"That wouldn't do me any good. I need you to retain mine. That way I'm representing an officer of the court, entitled to lawyer-client confidentiality, and in a position to demand to meet with an inmate in private. You wouldn't even have to be present."

"What could you gain there you couldn't in the visitors' room?"

"It's not what I'd gain, but what I'd lose. Namely a third party listening in."

"They can't do that."

I took my turn at smiling. "You've been out of criminal law a long time, Counselor. The Racketeer Influenced and Corrupt Organizations Act changed everything."

"What's RICO got to do with a domestic killing?"

"You know the system. The feds couldn't make a charge stick without throwing away the Bill of Rights, so they came up with a jump wire around it: They bug Catholic confessionals, suspend habeas corpus, stand the rule of law on its head by requiring the defense to prove innocence rather than the prosecution to prove guilt. It worked so swell they let the locals in on it. Since nine-eleven, all the lines are fuzzy. Someday somebody will take it all the way up to the Supreme Court, and if the right people are on the bench, we'll have something like justice back. But that won't happen between now and Saturday."

"My God, if what you say is true, how can you be sure your private conversation won't be bugged?"

"Let me worry about that." I waited. If what I'd said wasn't enough, nothing else I could come up with would be.

He sat in the same position a long time, resting on his forearms with his off-the-rack sport coat rucked up behind his neck. "And I should do this why?"

"If you don't know the answer to that, why did you agree to see me?"

"Curiosity."

"Bull. It wasn't your fault you were outmaneuvered in the courtroom. Innocent or not, Corbeil got a raw deal and it wasn't because you were inexperienced. If that didn't stick in your craw, you'd still be fighting the dirty fight in criminal procedure."

He nodded; not that it meant anything. "What do you charge?"

"You're in luck. Today's a holiday in Togo. I'm offering a special rate. Got a buck?"

He stroked a thumb across the button on his intercom, a twin of the one in the outer office; not to activate it. He seemed to be a man who liked to touch smooth things.

"How do I know if you can be trusted? Or if you're even who you say you are?"

I broke a card out of my wallet and passed it across the desk. It was embossed with the seal of the Detroit Police Department in blue and gold. "That's the extension of an inspector downtown. You can check the number online. We've known each other longer than we have anyone else." I got up.

He looked up from the card. "Where are you going?"

"Just outside. Fulsome praise embarrasses me."

The girl in the blue-black helmet jumped when I closed the door behind me. She was staring so hard at her screen she hadn't heard me entering. There didn't seem to be such of a much to look at, just a small piece of off-white crockery without a handle and some kind of insignia enameled on it in pale blue. Some anonymous party at eBay had sent her a message that someone had beaten her bid.

I placed a palm on her desk and bent closer to the monitor. "What's the prize?"

"Egg cup. I collect railroad china. This one came from the A, T, and SF. That's—"

"Atchison, Topeka, and the Santa Fe. I know the song. Aren't you the Pokémon generation?"

"My boyfriend says I have an old soul."

My inner child was older, but I said: "Too pricey?"

"I can afford twice the reserve. But this happens all the time.

Snipers swoop in and top me just before the auction closes. This office doesn't have the technology to compete."

"How long before closing?"

"Three minutes and change."

"Bid twice as much as you can afford."

"That's too risky. What if it's accepted?"

"So you skip lunch for a week. Only it won't go that high, and you'll have fun watching the snipers bomb out." I looked shame-faced. "I don't know Bill Gates from Buffalo Bill. A friend of mine uses the Net like a toy train, and I'm a good listener."

Her intercom buzzed. "That's me." I let myself back into the private office.

The thin smile was back behind the desk. "Are you sure you and this inspector are friends?"

"I didn't say that." I didn't sit.

"He asked what floor my office is on, and when I told him he said, 'No good, because five minutes after you come to an under-standing you'll want to throw him out a window.'"

"We kid," I said. "He's a kidder."

"He also said that if I didn't trust you I should be disbarred for criminal stupidity."

"He's a serious man."

He held out a tired-looking dollar. I relieved him of it and slipped it into my wallet.

"Do I get it back when Corbeil turns me down?"

A plastic stand on the desk displayed a sheath of his business cards. I helped myself to one. "If he does, I can use this to bluff my way in."

"They'll check."

I stared at him. His cheeks got pink. "Oh. Right."

We shook hands again.

The receptionist was beaming when I came out. "I got it, and for less than I budgeted. The pirate I was bidding against hit the wall three times before the horn! That was as much fun as getting the cup."

I grinned and gave her one of my cards. "Call me if there's a crack in it. I know a good lawyer."

THIRTEEN

I sat in the parking lot with my hands on the steering wheel, deciding whether to wait for Mihalich to make his pitch to Corbeil or head straight to the Huron Valley Men's Correctional Facility and try suckering my way in with the lawyer's card when my phone rang and it was Barry.

"Busy?" he said.

"Just plumbing the depths of the impossible. What you got?"

"Plenty, in person. Squat, over a cell. You're buying me lunch."

"Where?"

"Place called Carver's, on Winder. Know it?"

"I know Winder. When?"

"Now. I'm starving." He went away.

Restaurants have been pouring back into the city ever since it came out of bankruptcy. They've set up in vacant filling stations, lumber mills, warehouses, halfway houses, firehouses, churches, chop shops, storefronts, studios, scrapyards, and school buses; restaurants, in a pinch; but for the most part any extinct enterprise that never served up anything more edible than communion wafers. Carver's, at least, had selected a place in the food category. It occupied an old meatpacking plant, close enough to the Eastern Market to smell the onions that were destined to go with your steak if you dined there Saturday, still moist with earth. The new management had left the life-size poured-plaster cow grazing on the flat tar roof.

Under it, a local Rembrandt had decorated the cinder block front wall with a *trompe l'oeil* likeness of Hit City, U.S.A., the humble home of Motown Records, the label that launched a thousand swindles. The artist had an architect's eye for detail and no skill in basic anatomy: The figure leaning out one of the painted windows might have been Martha Reeves or Mushmouth. No one was paying me to find out what that had to do with dining out. A wooden sign shaped like an oversize meat cleaver hung by staples from a stanchion with CARVER'S scrawled on it in ragged letters, starting large and bold on the left and slanting to small and crabbed on the right, with dried paint spidering down from them like tear-streaked mascara. The effect was amateurish and stone-cold deliberate.

Spring rain started just as I pulled into a spot on the street two blocks down, blown at an angle from the direction of the river, a gift from Canada that never stops giving. It looked like tinsel and numbed my face like a backhand slap. I stood my collar on end and leaned into it. By the time I got to the entrance my eyelashes were as brittle as crystal stemware.

Dripping and waiting just inside the door for my eyes to grow accustomed to the change in light, I got a whiff of something that smelled more like a slaughterhouse than a place where meals are cooked and served. When my pupils caught up it looked like it smelled. Sides of meat hung from iron hooks slung by chains from the ceiling, rib cages exposed and glistening with blood still in the process of congealing. The room had the raw chill of a Michigan November. Commercial-grade reefers exhaled Freon with a hollow hiss from somewhere high on the walls. At a long butcher block table, a corps in paper hats and spattered aprons armed with steel cleavers and blue-edged knives cut loins of beef and pork into thick slabs and paper-thin slices, the blades gliding through gristle and bone like lasers.

A black muscular party in a spotless white T-shirt and ducks spotted me from his post at the end of the table, where he'd stood supervising the operation with tattooed arms crossed, and hastened my way, swaying from side to side in a sailor's roll.

"I'm sorry, sir. We're closed."

I said, "Somebody gave me a bum steer, so to speak. I was told this was a restaurant."

"It is, but we don't open till six." He crossed his arms again. A teal-colored mermaid popped her pink nipples on his right biceps.

"I'm meeting someone. Blond guy with a Dutch leg."

"What's a Dutch leg?"

"Something you might get if you lose your grip on your cleaver."

"Oh, him." The arms dropped to his sides. A head that could have worn a scalding cauldron for a hat tilted toward a door at the back, rough oak planking with iron bands.

The atmosphere changed abruptly on the other side. Round-backed chairs perched upside-down on circular oak tables polished to a soft shine under bowl fixtures suspended by chains from heavy beams. A horseshoe-shaped bar separated the dining room from rows of glass bottles and cut-crystal lit softly from behind like a display of expensive perfume. Barry Stackpole sat at the only table that was dressed for business, with silver setups and linen napkins on white cloth. A squat faceted glass stood at his elbow. I drew out the chair opposite him and sat. As I did so I caught a gust of brandy and triple sec.

"Sidecar," I said. "A little early for you."

"Not for you. A guy your age shouldn't drink alone."

He looked more collegiate than usual in a white V-neck sweater with gold Chief Justice Rehnquist stripes on the arms over a soft burgundy flannel shirt; Archie Andrews imbibing on a fake ID. We shared the place with a female bartender, who came over and asked what I wanted to drink. She was dressed for off-duty in sweatpants and a Red Wings jersey, with her brown hair twisted into a ponytail. She didn't look old enough to drink a cocktail legally, much less mix and serve one.

I looked at Barry. "I thought you were starving."

"I am. I ordered a Reuben. It pays to get in early here, like at the airport."

"Sorry about the slow service," the bartender said. "The cook had to stoke up the stove and the waitstaff comes on at five. Mr. Stackpole caught us with our pants down." It was hard to tell from her expression if she was kidding or sore.

I said, "I'll have the same."

"And to drink?"

"Same also, only leave out the lemon juice and liqueur."

"Just brandy then."

"If you want to get technical."

"Separate checks?"

I said no.

"What do you think of the place?" Barry asked when she left.

"In here's okay. Out front it looks, smells, and feels like Jeffrey Dahmer's basement."

"Worst culinary mistake since they installed a king-size replica of the human alimentary canal in the U of M Hospital cafeteria. The owner's under the impression Detroiters like things real. Only Detroiters are too smart to fall for impressions. I give it six months."

"How do you rate special service?"

"I got him a spread in *Hour Detroit*. He sank fifty grand in the joint. Rumor is that's what changed hands when Whitey Bulger was killed. I figured anyone who rendered that kind of community service deserved a break. Best corned beef in the city. Point cut; none of that extra-lean wet sawdust for me."

"Still quivering, no doubt."

The bartender brought my drink. I waited until she returned to her station. "What'd Kopernick do that stuck him in a doghouse so bad he had to come to me to get him out?"

"It's not as juicy as the Reuben, but juicy enough. You remember that casino suicide last year?"

"Which one would that be?"

"Funny; but it's rare. Usually they stew over it at home for a day or so, but this one happened on the spot. Off-duty cop dumped a bundle at blackjack and shot himself at the table. It happened at Motor City."

"I must've been out of town. Score zero for the metal detectors."

"A patron at the same table gave him CPR, but he wasted his breath of life. The slug had plowed a path from the roof of the mouth to the back of the skull, which is where it came to a much-deserved rest. Anyway the Good Samaritan bought him fifteen minutes till the EMT arrived, so he got to be a hero about as long as you did after the bank job."

"At a guess, Kopernick was the Samaritan."

"Probably the first time he got to use it since training, or wanted to."

Our meals came, steaming hot on black bread with pickle spears and battered fries. I was hungrier than I thought. I took a bite before asking the obvious. "So what's the jam?"

"He was on duty, and it wasn't his beat."

"Ah. Sticky wicket when the department needs the good press."

A fork poked at a pile of fries distractedly. His starvation seemed to have passed. "There's no press in this town. If there were, they wouldn't accept the crime figures the chief hands out every January. In my day we kept our own count. And we kept asking questions until the official version of a deal blew out like a cheap recap. Anyway, Stan the Man's eighteen months away from his thirty. What are the odds in all that time he won't trip over his own flabby brain and wind up checking names against a clipboard in the lobby of the Penobscot Building?"

"About the same as the building standing that long." I used some of my brandy. "So the part of Kopernick's brain that's not so flabby tells him he needs to put his face in front of a gang of cameras on a prominent homicide case. That way the city's looking the other way when he trips."

"The theory fits the facts. The facts being he's up against it major league or he'd never go to you for the boost."

"Thanks, Barry. Tell 'em to poleax dessert on me."

"How you gonna play it?"

"Right down the middle, like Pickett's Charge."

"Statue of Liberty play? You?"

"Why not? You can only make an end run so many times before they catch on."

"Still think you can turn Kopernick into a double agent?"

"Maybe. Also I'm getting brittle in my senior years. I can use a big strapping fellow to help me across the street."

"And drop you down an open manhole."

He ate half his corned beef and got a container for the rest when the ponytailed bartender came back with the bill. "The homeless guy who hangs out in the alley will appreciate this," he said, scooping it into Styrofoam. "He's Irish."

Back out in the charnel house the team was slicing side meat off a hog, parting the white flesh with long straight sweeps like a scythe. The man with the tattoos greeted us with a tortured smile; it was close enough to the dinner hour to put on his evening manners. He asked if we enjoyed our meal.

I said, "Okay, only I'm a vegetarian now."

The rain had turned to sleet, rattling against the pavement like dice in a cup and stinging the back of my neck like yellowjackets. Of course the sun shone throughout, the sadistic son of a bitch.

I drove back to my building to crunch the brain. I got part of it done on the way, but thinking without result is like labor without accomplishment: It doesn't count as work, only waste.

I was still at it halfway up the stairs before the character loitering in the foyer registered.

He'd stood with his back to me, reading the wall directory. If I knew him at all, it was as one of a couple of hundred people I'd met who left no more impression than a foot in a slush puddle; after all, how much can you get from a man's back? But it was just another reminder that I'd lost ground. Time was when I'd have braced him for taking up space in a part of the building that was designed just to walk across on the way to somewhere else. That year I was sharing the building with a webmaster for a mail-order warehouse, a designer of corrective footwear, a rookie wedding planner, and a floral consultant; no one worth stalking, just me.

At the second-floor landing I turned and went back down, stepping up the pace as if I'd forgotten something in the car. He was gone by then, of course. Why should both of us ignore our instincts?

FOURTEEN

S omehow I knew the phone would ring. I'm only psychic about
that when it's a call I'd rather not take.

Waiting for it gave me time to think about the groundhog
in the foyer who'd ducked out when he saw his shadow. I cranked
my feet up onto the drawleaf and walked a cigarette across the back
of my hand, a parlor trick I'd learned in the old neighborhood. I
took up smoking just so I could show it off. I was young then and
almost as stupid as I am now.

He didn't have to have anything to do with the current job. In
my time I'd drawn an entourage as long as Michael Jordan's, if a
hell of a lot less glamorous; but not lately. The last three assign-
ments had been in the nature of credit checks and deadbeat loans,
quick-money deals I'd put away over the phone, nothing worth
sprinkling salt on my tail. If it was the Goss deal, maybe it meant
I wasn't just spinning my wheels after all; be nice if someone would
tell me what I was doing right so I could keep on doing it.

On the other hand, the guy might just have wandered into the
wrong building.

Just that moment the bell jarred me out of my little sortie into
self-delusion. It made me jump, same as if I hadn't been expecting
it. I picked up, and sure enough the voice was that flabby baritone
that sounded like a bear coming out of hibernation.

"So we partners or what?" it said.

I put my feet on the floor. They were going to sleep anyway. "One condition, Detective. We keep each other posted on our plans so we don't wind up walking on each other's heels, and we meet to compare notes, not just when something breaks."

"I'm down with that, like the kids say. This ain't no buddy film. So what's next for you?"

"Show me yours first."

"That don't seem fair."

"You came to me, Kopernick. There's an order to these things."

"Okay. Just now I'm in the basement at the Second, collecting dust bunnies in my ears, catching up with Dan Corbeil, April Goss, and George W. Bush. When a case has been buried this long, you got to back up in order to go forward. Your turn."

"Not yet. You should enroll your stooges in a remedial reading course. It doesn't take more than thirty seconds to read five names on a building directory."

"Hang on, son. I feel like I just walked in at half-time and I don't know who's playing."

I told him about my fraternal twin downstairs.

"You better get your house in order," he said. "Why would I tranquilize and tag you when we were going to work together anyway?"

"You didn't know that until just now. I never knew a cop of your type that didn't wear suspenders and a belt."

"Shame on you for peekin'. Only you're barking down the wrong hole this time. If I *was* to pin a tail on you, I'd pin it so it stayed pinned, at least till he got his teeth into something. I ain't just sure I don't resent being called stupid more than I do getting accused of a double cross."

"Okay, so it wasn't you."

"I don't give a rat's ass if you think so or if you don't; but if it keeps you from messing your pants I can put a man on your man and play a little handball with him."

"I can do that myself, and it won't get me in any worse jam downtown than usual. That's more than I can say for you."

There was a thump on his end. I didn't think he'd keeled over in a dead faint. Probably he'd dumped the load of papers he was going through on a work table. He coughed up a lungful of desiccated paper and eraser shavings. "I guess I don't know what in Christ's name you're talking about."

"I'm guessing you do. How'd you make out at the blackjack table?"

"Well, ain't this place just as leaky as the White House. Who you been talking to?"

"Does it matter, if there's as many holes as that?" I swiped the grin off my face; I'd enjoyed that more than expected. And to think I'd almost kept my mouth shut.

"I'm not putting the boots to you, Detective. In a department that can't keep track of its rape kits and treats the evidence room like it's Trader Joe's, a cop playing hooky to turn a few cards doesn't raise so much as a scratch in my throat. If we're going to partner up, we can't have any secrets about why. Truth to tell, I never trusted you as much as I did once I found out about you and Motor City. You know why I'm working this case; now I know why you are. The way I see it, that makes us Turner and Hooch."

Paper rustled. He'd returned to his homework. "Okay." It wasn't, but a diesel bull is nothing if not a realist. "Just so long as I'm Tom Hanks and not the flea factory. What you got?"

I told him about my arrangement with Mihalich. Paper kept crackling.

"Two clients, one case," he said. "Ain't that a conflict of interest?"

"Not when they both want the same thing. I'm only taking money from one, and it's a fire sale at that."

"You just said you needed the lawyer to get Corbeil's cooperation. That don't sound like he and little sister want the same thing."

"Baby steps. If I can get him to let her continue with the investigation, and I can prove he didn't kill anyone, it'll sure enough be the same thing when he walks out that gate."

"You're sold, then. Danny boy's a pigeon."

"I didn't say that; but with the amount of circumstantial evidence the state had against him, going to all that trouble, suppressing the results of the pregnancy exam, seems like more than just gilding the lily. Why tilt the pinball machine when you've racked up ten thousand points? Someone didn't have faith in the odds. Someone who already knew the system, too."

"Someone being Chester Goss."

"He's my guy for now. As April's father, he'd be emotionally invested in seeing her killer brought to justice enough to go beyond all reason. And even back then he had enough weight to throw around to make it stick."

"He's got a hell of a lot more now. Enough to nuke your license and run me out of every department in the country."

"Well, if you're scared—"

"Sure I'm scared. I'm scared every time I'm first through the door in a crack house, but I go through anyhow, and I got one hell of a lot more to lose there. Just now I'm just assessing risk, and from where I sit it sure don't look so bad as that. I just thought I'd mention it so you'd know. Now you brought up the problem, how are you gonna handle it?"

"You've got your pronouns mixed up."

"Huh?"

I'd forgotten he was homeschooled.

"Not me. You."

He was slower on the draw than I remembered; his neck on the block was impairing his instincts. I gave up waiting. "I'm saying make noise about looking into the Goss case. Force him to show his hand."

"That's department policy! I don't have the pull to reopen an investigation. If I ever had, I sure as hell wouldn't have it after last year."

"Who knows about that, outside the department? I'm not saying you make it official. Just drop the hint around the department. A junior crime-stopper like Goss is bound to have some pets downtown."

"Shame on you," he said. "The G-men flushed all the bad apples out of here years ago."

I stopped juggling the cigarette and set fire to it. It burned halfway down to the filter; that airing had dried it out like King Tut. I squashed it in the tray.

"You said that with a straight face. Okay, maybe you're not just rehearsing for your press conference, and all your colleagues are happy serving the public for peanuts. Maybe they're just starstruck, think Goss will give 'em their own TV show. All I know is, from what I've seen of his, he doesn't get all his dope from the public record. If it breaks right, you'll be out of the hole and then some."

"If it breaks right; and even if it don't. The chief'll give the collar to one of *his* pets and bust me for telling tales out of school."

"Not if you beat him to it. You had friends in the press when you worked the April Goss case the first time. If you didn't still have some, that CPR story wouldn't have survived the Early Edition. The chief already climbed out on a limb when he let the casino business slide. He covered for you then, he'll do it again when you bring in a trophy."

I could hear dust motes settling in the basement of the Second Precinct. Then:

"You sure got guts. I guess it's just my hard luck they're all mine."

"You wanted in. I'm not offering free partnerships today."

"Only on your end. I walk this plank, where's yours?"

"Right next door," I said, "and it's a hell of a lot shorter. I took the first step when I agreed to stir ashes the department threw water on three presidents back. You of all people should know a cold case is city property always and forever, no civilians need apply."

"You're used to it. Gimme a minute before I make up my mind to kick the stool out from under me."

"Take two. I'm easy."

His tone went down a full octave. He was probably alone in the basement, but I could see him hunkered close to the table, wrapping his body like a tent all the way around the conversation.

"You better not be peddling the Ambassador Bridge. We got a rocky record, you and me."

"What are pals for?"

"Cut the crap just for once. I find out you dug me a trap, all they'll ever find of you is a grease slick clear down to Toledo. You think I'm just being colorful, you ain't been paying attention."

"You take care too, Detective." I dropped the receiver back into its cradle.

The sun was back, this time leaving behind the rest of the weather. I swung to the window and held up both hands, one above the other, palms toward me, measuring its commute to the western suburbs; it involved less effort than turning my swivel eight inches to read the wall clock. Two hours to quitting—if I had a job that let me go at five.

It was time to check with lawyer Mihalich to see if he'd made any progress with Corbeil. When I picked up the handset, a string of beeps told me I had a message on voice mail; I'd added the feature to my landline in the thin hope that two people might want to be in touch with me at the same time. It was from Mihalich; life should be like that more often.

"I just got off the phone with our man in Ypsi. He's on board, and I've notified the staff to that effect."

My watch said I had a couple hours before visiting closed at Huron Valley. I slid into an all-weather coat, just in time for the sky to clear.

I caught a flash of a figure in my side-view mirror as I was climbing behind the wheel; that was pure accident. I was in the middle of swinging the door shut. By the time I turned to look out the rear window, the figure was gone.

That couldn't be coincidence. Even in Detroit, people with nothing to hide don't duck out of sight that quick. A narrow alley separated the struggling micro-brewery where I parked and the abandoned mini–police station next door—a lingering hangover from the Murder City years—was barely wide enough for two cats to pass simultaneously, but someone in a hurry to be invisible would find it handy.

I could have run after him. I didn't. I'd gotten a glimpse of a horse face, a brown Fu Manchu moustache that looked like tobacco spittle, shaggy hair the color of rust streaks on cinder block, and a filthy gray hoodie sagging like wash from a wire hanger. It might as well have belonged to the loiterer in the foyer as to anyone. I'd know it next time.

Throttling the big 255 into life, I had a snap of recognition. It was there and gone, like a single frame in a movie, and afterward I wasn't anywhere near sure. The more I thought about it the more convinced I was I was wrong.

You can get nuts turning that one over and over, like a half-familiar melody, so I shoved it behind my frontal lobe. But for a fraction of time I thought I'd seen him somewhere that wasn't my building or my mirror.

FIFTEEN

There it was again; but then I'd hardly expected it not to be, bearing a closer resemblance to a medical clinic than the clink, if you subtracted the hoops of razor wire and the rows of police growlers and armored vans parked in the restricted zone; at that hour the sun turned the windows into sheets of metal, masking the bars. I slid in beside a glandular case of a Dodge Ram jacked up on tractor tires, with the double horses' heads of the International Brotherhood of Teamsters pasted to the girder-like rear bumper. That made it a guard's personal ride. In that neighborhood my muscle car looked like a case of TB.

Before getting out I unpinned the honorary deputy's star from my ID folder and stowed it in the glove compartment. I only kept it to balance out my wallet in the opposite pocket; it wouldn't fool a reality-show host and only teed off the authorities. I'd left the small arms in the safe. At that point I didn't think it would be of any use in a homicide case that was old enough to vote. At that point.

The prison had a different protocol for private visitors. The female guard in the booth directed me down a hall to an office whose door stood open. There a young man in uniform sat at a steel desk with a laptop on it. Whatever kind of chair he was using was concealed by an ass as big as a diving bell. He looked at my ID, rattled his keyboard, read what came up, and nodded. From a drawer he took a wand like the ones the TSA personnel use at the airport.

That was a relief. I was afraid he was going to take out a rubber glove.

He braced a hand on the desk, his face reddening, and got up with a woof. The vinyl cushioned seat on his chair let out a long windy sigh like a mule when its packs are unloaded.

I set what I'd carried in on the floor, emptied my pockets of wallet, change, and keys, put them on the desk, and assumed the cruciform position. He finished with the wand and put it away. He sat back down, making the same sound as the cushion had, and pointed a bratwurst finger at the object on the floor. It was the size and shape of a football helmet with a folding handle on top.

"What's that?"

"CD player. It comes back out with me when I leave. I thought he could use the entertainment."

He hoisted it onto what passed for his lap and spent ten minutes examining it inside and out. He removed the CD, looked at both sides, put it back, opened the battery compartment, plucked out four AAs, and gave each the same treatment. He put everything back and held it out.

Five minutes after he spoke to someone on the phone, another turnkey came to the door and looked me over as thoroughly as his colleague had the CD player. This one was Indian or Pakistani, with eyes as hard as walnuts and a chronic five o'clock shadow. Guard Dumbo's uniform would have made three of his.

I had to trot to keep up with him as we passed down a series of taupe-painted corridors—walls, floor, ceiling, the works, the identical dishwater color you get mixing any combination of paint in existence—with nothing on the walls. It was so monotonous it was damn near hallucinogenic.

Just as I started to wish I'd brought along peanut shells to mark the trail, we turned yet another corner into a short hallway that dead-ended at a blank steel security door, painted the same color; if you weren't paying attention you'd walk right into it. He swiped his ID through the slot. A buzzer sounded and the door unlatched itself with a clunk.

He opened it, stood aside for me to go through, then followed, letting the door close on its pneumatic sausage. That was when the Huron Valley Men's Correctional Center looked less like a hospital complex and every bit like a penitentiary from a studio backlot. The room was a hundred-yard rectangle, two stories tall, and stacked to the ceiling with tiers of cells. Troughs of fluorescent tubes washed it in bright light and the concrete floor was polished to a high shine. From the white-enameled bars of the cells to the catwalk that separated the tiers, the place was as clean as a cotton swab. Guards armed with folding batons walked the floor and catwalk, and a sharpshooter manned a corner balcony twenty feet up cradling a scoped rifle. Every scrape of a sole or clink of keys echoed. The place was an amphitheater.

Apart from that it was as quiet as anywhere on earth.

We took a flight of gridded steel steps to the second tier and passed along the cells there at that same busy clip. The occupants had managed to find some gloom inside the cages, or maybe they created their own; aside from the occasional fists gripping the bars and forearms resting on the crossbars, hands dangling outside in the only freedom they knew, they were shadows only. It wasn't a sadistic guard or the hard labor or even the threat of a shower-room rape that gnawed and gnawed at human hope; it was the crushing boredom.

I didn't make eye contact. I'd seen *The Silence of the Lambs* too many times.

The block guards watched us, paying particular attention to the CD player. Time dragged for them too, and any wrinkle in the routine was worth looking at.

We came to a cell near the end, where the Asian officer rapped his knuckles on steel. "You've got a visitor. Stand back from the bars, hands behind you."

It was the first time he'd spoken. Instead of the singsong cadence of tech-support, his accent was pure Chicago, hard and flat as a manhole cover.

A figure stretched out on a cot swung its feet to the floor and did as commanded. The guard rattled a fistful of brass keys on a ring the size of a tennis ball and twisted one in the lock. He opened the door and gave me just enough room to step in past him. He remained facing the prisoner.

"Sing out when you're ready."

The door crashed shut. That sound never failed to scramble up my spine.

The architect who designed the first modern prison cell could loan money to a Saudi royal, if he were entitled to dividends: standard eight-by-ten, steel corner sink, steel toilet without a lid, steel bunk bolted to the floor to discourage the occupant from picking it up and swinging it at a guard's head, no second-story bunk; Michigan law prohibits more than one to a cell. It's promoted as humane, but the state legislator who'd introduced the bill was probably a man with a wife, kids, and five in-laws in residence. In the long history of incarceration, not one suicide had taken place in the presence of a cellmate. At least, not unassisted.

He took his hands from behind him and sat on the edge of the bunk, feet apart and his hands on his thighs. His eyes glittered under their heavy lids. In the dim light from outside the cell his skin was gray-white.

He glanced at the CD player I'd put on the floor, said nothing. Twenty years of being told what to do and not asking why had burned all the curiosity out of him. That was the major takeaway when you left the joint; if you left it. One more thing you'd never get back.

"You know why I'm here," I said.

Nothing moved in his face. "Sure. Prison telegraph; Morse code knocked out on the plumbing. How many movies have you seen?"

I ducked the question. "Guards' gossip. They make the Joy Luck Club look like the CIA. Also procedure. You had to sign off on the agreement. Why?"

"Chrys."

"She spoke to you?"

"No. I knew she was behind it. I was pretty rough on her last time. Throw her a bone, you know?"

I had him then; his soft spot. It takes a lot of character to hang on to one after so much time.

"It'll take me a while to come through on that thing you asked," I said. "About the drainage system here. Bureaucracy."

He was Buddha for a solid minute. Then his lips peeled apart in that same way I remembered. Didn't he say even a word to his inmates?

"Thanks for coming."

I let half a second pass. It was a beginning. "I was in the neighborhood." Even a lukewarm response can break the ice.

"Tell you truth, it was getting kind of dull around here."

I grinned. Even when I grin in a mirror it comes back. Not in this case.

"What do they do around here now, anyway?" I said. "I guess they don't break rocks. India's nailed down the textile racket, Washington's farmed out license plates to China. You might be laid off anytime."

He sat solid.

I leaned back against the bars, hands in my pockets. "There's activity in your case. I've got the first responder at the crime scene on board."

"*What* crime?"

That threw me for a second; but long-time isolation can lead to dementia. I started to remind him of the details of the investigation. He cut me off; first time he'd shown aggression.

"April killed herself. They say that's illegal, but if it's successful it's the perfect crime."

There was a spark of life in his face then, but as far as it went I might have galvanized a frog, jerking a limb from pure electric shock. There was nothing of actual life in it.

I leaned down and switched on the CD player. "Hope you like recorded books."

"Why?" He raised his voice over the jabber coming from the speakers.

I shushed him. I leaned in close and kept my voice even. You can make yourself heard in a hurricane once you find the level. I waved a hand around the cell. "The walls have ears—maybe. The Justice Department decided it couldn't win, so it kicked over the board."

It was a John Grisham novel; something about a courageous lawyer fighting a corrupt system, read by the current Hollywood flash in a monotone that could put the Tasmanian devil to sleep. A skilled techie might be able to record and untangle our conversation from the reading, but it would take time and cost plenty. I didn't think even Chester Goss would foot the bill.

"So I'm government property now?" Corbeil said. "I thought I only killed a coed."

He was a fast learner. He'd keyed his volume down to match mine, just under the celebrity's core decibel. It was kind of like communicating over a lower frequency; half vocal, half lip-reading.

It was silly as hell. He was right: No one would be listening in on a twenty-year-old domestic murder. But strings had been pulled on this one, and they might still have had some tensile strength in them.

"Did April Goss tell you she might not be pregnant?"

He showed emotion for the first time, if twin streaks of copper on his cheeks were any indication. Apart from that the muscles in his face might have been cured in salt. "You went to all this trouble to ask me that? Read the report! It must be in public domain after all this time, like *Moby-Dick*!"

"I need a refresher. The fact that it was suppressed from evidence may be the key that springs you. Answer the question. What've you got to lose?"

He looked down at his hands. The fingers were tying themselves into knots and he seemed to wonder what they had to secure. Then he looked up. His eyes were dull under the bloated lids.

"I never heard a word about it till the trial."

"Did Mihalich know?"

"Ask him."

"I will. I would have when I saw him, but I was too busy convincing him to take you back on. The point I'm making is if the prosecution sprang it in the courtroom without letting the defense in on it in Discovery, it could have been used to appeal the verdict and get you another chance in court."

He blinked. Otherwise his expression didn't change. It's one of the first survival tactics you learn in the penal system.

"Mihalich didn't object at the time," he said. "That much I remember."

"He was green then. That's why public defenders come so cheap. After all this time, though, an oversight like that isn't likely to draw much water."

"Then why go into it?"

"Block by block, that's how you build a case. You had to have found out later that the fact that she wasn't pregnant after all was kept from the jury. Someone went to a lot of trouble and probably expense to make sure it didn't come up. Mihalich could have raised the issue that you knew she wasn't—the other side couldn't prove you didn't—and that would've blown holes in the case against you. Convictions have been made without establishing a motive, but with an experienced defense attorney in charge, a hung jury and a mistrial is a strong possibility."

He'd been sitting with his palms on his knees. He leaned back against the wall, drawing them up to his thighs, leaving wet patches on his prison denims. That was a breakthrough. Before that his sweat glands might have dried up and turned to dust for all he made use of them.

"What you're saying is I might have swung a new trial based on my lawyer's incompetence. You do know you're working for him."

"And he knows he wasn't equipped to handle a major homicide case while the ink was still wet on his diploma. That's why he agreed to take you back on. Dan, that brings the people on your side up to three."

"Swell. Now all we have to do is convince the attorney general, the governor, and every goddamn player in the twenty-four-hour news cycle."

My game leg had gone to sleep and the bars I was leaning against were digging furrows in my back. I straightened, sending electrical impulses tingling down my thigh, and put my hands in my pockets. Grinned.

"Piece of cake," I said. "Until I came into this cage, Team Corbeil didn't even have Corbeil. Once you've put fight in the patient, the disease don't stand a chance."

"Try peddling that in the prison cemetery."

I let him have that one. It was pretty good, at that.

He said, "So that's what you came here to accomplish? Cheer me up so you can keep gouging my baby sister?"

"I'll be lucky if I make expenses on this one. When Goss gets wind I'm still on it, he'll crank the heat up so high it'll make global warming look like the last ice age."

"Then what's your end?"

"I'm a sucker for a good joke."

He started to get mad; the breakthroughs were coming one on top of another, like fish swimming up the rapids. "You think this is funny?"

"Not yet. So far all I've got is the setup: 'Guy walks into a bank . . .'"

SIXTEEN

Our rush hours aren't calculated in terms of time. The auto plants change shifts on a staggered schedule, carving the heavy traffic periods into quarters, thirds, halves of each day; the windows of opportunity are narrow and largely a matter of luck. I was shoehorning my way into the stream of assembly line workers from Ypsilanti and Rawsonville when my cell rang. I recognized Kopernick's number. We were phone pals now.

I took one hand off the wheel just long enough to answer and activate the speaker. A wall of tractor-trailer rigs had me in the center of a rolling canyon and the tension cramped my knuckles and ran a stiff rod up my back.

"Something." The cop wasn't much for hellos. "Got a hot date tonight?"

"Not since Bush forty-one. Where and when?"

"Better write it down. Place we're meeting, addresses don't count."

"Give me time to pull over. I'm in the mixing bowl." I rang off, found my opening, and scraped out of the pocket between a Corrigan Oil tanker and a cattle truck. That gave me ten seconds to change lanes again and knock a corner off the exit onto Washtenaw Avenue. I keep the monster engine tuned up; by the time the horns responded they were whispers in my wake. I coasted into a convenience store lot and found a space around the corner of the building where the employees parked. Got out my pad and pen and called him back. "Shoot," I said. "That's just an expression, Detective."

"Screw you." He gave me the directions, as fast as I could take them down in my bastard shorthand. They weren't nearly as complicated as a scavenger hunt in Borneo.

"You're sure this is in Detroit?" I said when he stopped.

"Used to be. Seven-thirty." And he was gone.

By the time I got back to the suburbs I'd recovered enough from my Carver's experience to chance chili con carne and a beer on tap at the place in Southfield, but Claire was off duty and the waitress I got mixed up my order. I settled for tomato soup and a can of Miller Lite. You can't go home again.

From what little I could draw from the directions Kopernick had given me, the neighborhood didn't dress for dinner. I stopped home long enough to change into a turtleneck, corduroys, and a leather windbreaker, all in grays and browns, which blend into darkness better than cat-burglar black. When it came time to accessorize, I hesitated over my veteran Chief's Special, then put it in a drawer, took down the Ruger Blackhawk from the top shelf of the closet, checked the cylinder, and strapped the woven nylon holster to my belt. Packing a piece is never comfortable, but the Magnum felt like a bootheel against my kidney. Maybe it was how I'd come by it and who gave it to me. But something about the place I was headed told me I might need more firepower than the .38.

After seven in early spring, Detroit from the air looks like a spill of costume jewelry with black patches in it, like blank spots on a medieval map. The lighted sections are safer than the dark, but unless you're looking down from above, you don't know you've wandered into a potential cancer spot until you're tangled in shadow. Trust a Morlock like Stan Kopernick to stake out one of those for a meet. I drove around a four-block radius three times looking for the place. I'd lived all my adult life in the city, but where

I was supposed to be that night might have been smuggled in from North Korea for all I recognized it.

Finally I pulled over to a curb that had half deteriorated into a dirt berm, fished the pencil flash out of the glove compartment, and re-read the directions from the start. When I looked up again through the window on the passenger's side, the spill from the flash reflected off a triangle of broken glass; what was left of a window in a building as dark as the night behind it, and invisible except for that dusty glow.

I got out and locked up, taking the flash. There wasn't a star in sight; maybe none ever visited that street. It wasn't even a street, really: The cracked pavement ended fifty yards from the corner in a cement wall supporting the Fisher Freeway. The house—if it was a house—was the only one on that stretch of asphalt.

The grass in front, where it wasn't leaning over every which way, was almost waist high and sopping with dew. Before stepping that direction I bent down and pulled my socks up over my pants cuffs. That might confuse some of the chiggers long enough to let me pass.

Rats were something else. The city turns them out on a conveyor, like cars, too many to know fear of man. I aimed the flash at the ground ahead and swept the beam from side to side. It glinted off shattered glass, found enough used condoms to skip a generation, and at least one pair of red eyes that dared me to approach before they turned and withdrew on tiny unhurried feet.

My toe struck something solid. I jumped—it could be a wine jug or a human rib cage—and stabbed at it with the beam. It was a twisted length of tarnished steel ending in a rectangle with block letters peering through a rash of rust:

H TI GS

Some sharpshooter had punched out three of the letters with rounds big enough to choke a frog, but a student of regional history hardly needed them to fill in the blanks.

Hastings: a collector's item, that sign. That truncated chunk of street might have been all that was left of one of the most sinister neighborhoods in town. After decades of snipings, rapes, drug murders, and domestic wars, City Hall had eliminated the problem the way it did most of the others: demolished it to make way for a freeway. The thrum of passing traffic belonged to a planet in some other galaxy.

I'd stood in one spot too long. Something pricked an ankle, burning like a red-hot needle. I hoped it wasn't a plague flea. I stooped and struck at it with the flash. That only barked the shin. I continued forward at a brisker pace, all the while sweeping the path for rats and snakes. I kept the flash pointed down to let my eyes adjust to the gloom.

A slab of crumbling concrete stood in for a front porch. I mounted it and trained the light on a door spray-painted with a gang sign and someone's idea of social expression; FUCK is a hard word to misspell, but he'd managed. The place was a house, all right, a mid-century saltbox sided with asbestos tile. No illumination came from inside. Detroit Edison would have forgotten the address long ago, and if it was serving currently as a crack house—another local industry, like breeding rats—the oil lamps weren't burning. There was a lamppost on the corner, but no city employee was coming to that neighborhood to replace a burned-out bulb.

I tried the door; it opened inward with no more resistance than grit on the hinges.

That stopped me for a second. I don't care for unlocked doors, not where I live. They'd led me into deadfall traps more than once. The Ruger came out. I snapped off the flash, put it away, and followed the revolver over the threshold.

Spring nights are rarely warm in Michigan. They're colder still when trapped in a damp enclosure with no light. I nudged the door shut with a heel and stepped to the side, putting a solid wall between me and the grayer dark of outside.

But even pupils slowing with age couldn't miss a cigar-end glowing in the dark at the far end of the room. I cocked the Ruger. In that black hole on the back side of civilization, the noise was almost as loud as a blast from the barrel.

SEVENTEEN

A match cracked and flared yellow, illuminating only the broad planes of a great slab of face. Something slid with a grating sound and the sharp stench of kerosene pierced my nostrils. Greasy orange light spread from an oil lamp, forming a lopsided circle a foot and a half in diameter. The glass chimney grated back into place over the burning wick.

Stan Kopernick blew out the match, dropped it on the floor, and puffed on his cigar. The smoke was silvery in the meager glow. The light didn't quite reach the brim of his hat, leaving a strip of shadow there with his eyes glistening through. He was sitting in a mohair-upholstered armchair with stuffing billowing out of it like steam from a locomotive.

"You took your own sweet time getting here."

I took the Ruger off cock and put it away. "Not so sweet," I said, "and not my own. I sold it to a client. I had to hire a time machine to find the place. Where's yours?"

"Around the corner, under a light. Those unmarked units are candy to carjackers. You'll be lucky if yours is still waiting for you."

"That's why I camouflage it with dents and rust. Why here? Siberia too far?"

"That ain't just rotten wood and rat turds you're smelling. It's history. They ought to put a brass plaque on the place. What do you know about the Black Legion?"

I lit a cigarette. The stink of history was getting to me. "Klan offshoot," I said, stepping on the match. "Thirties or thereabout. They burn a cross here or what?"

"Nothing so gaudy. They tried a guy for being colored without a license: Set up a table for the judge's bench, folding chairs for the jury, Confederate flag, the works. Twelve bad men and false deliberated without leaving the room. The bailiff and the sergeant-at-arms drove the poor son of a bitch clear out to Melvindale and shot him by the salt mines. Those days there weren't as many empty lots as now.

"Even yellow-bellies had some guts," he said. "They set up court right here in the middle of the Black Bottom; what the locals called Paradise Valley. That's like organizing a Nazi bund rally in Tel Aviv. Not that brass balls did them any good when they stood trial for real. Doing life in Michigan can make you beg for the chair."

"Charming story. You should be a tour guide. The urban explorers would want to know about this place; they love to play Indiana Jones. I don't see you for the part. Why meet here, and not the Second? I left my cloak and dagger at home."

"It's practically the only place in town without a working surveillance camera or a busybody next door." He blew a ragged ring of smoke. "I got a call from Chester Goss a couple of hours ago."

I dropped the butt and crushed it out. "You and I only got hitched this afternoon. His pipeline into the department must be top-grade copper. Excuse the play on words."

He let that one slide. It wasn't that good anyway. "Who needs a pipeline? Plumbing's already full of holes. He offered me a job: consulting expert, assigned to his show with a personal service contract, benefits and all."

"He can be charming," I said after a moment. "When we met he told me all about how he'd looked up his heritage and took up a sport connected with it. Then when he found out what I was there for he threw me out. What I'm saying is he might not be the best boss in the world."

"Thought you'd try to talk me out of it."

"I'm nobody's guardian angel; just figured you'd like to know the facts, one working stiff to another." I rolled a shoulder. "Congratulations. He could've saved himself a bundle with just an envelope of cash."

He drew on the cigar, hard enough for the end to spread its glow to his hat brim. It might have been responsible for the angry flush; you can't be sure where a man like Kopernick's concerned. Anyway when he spoke his tone was even. "I got a job I like. This one sounds like there's a lot of reading involved."

"Turn it down?"

"Told him I'd talk it over with the wife."

"You surprise me."

"That a lowlife like me don't jump at the easy buck?"

"That you've got a wife. I thought you lived in an efficiency apartment with a direct line to Escorts R Us."

"She's a trooper. When the chief threatened me with a month's unpaid suspension for that thing in the casino, I had to talk her out of marching downtown with a rolling pin. She probably wouldn't be so loyal if I told her I dropped an investigation in return for a warm spot on a windowsill. I bought some time to let you know. You and me promised each other we'd come running whenever something broke."

I dealt myself another butt. I didn't want it; one of the few advantages of being a tobacco addict is all the business involved gives you time to access your brain cells. I'd invested too much time in hating Detective First-Grade Stan Kopernick to start just disliking him now.

Unless he was running the tired old game. I hadn't the energy to work out the odds. I flipped a mental coin. It stood on end.

"He's scared," I said; "Goss is. I call that progress."

He blew a plume of smoke and tapped a half-inch of ash onto the floor. It had seen worse, if what he'd said about the Black Legion wasn't just theater. "Putting aside the possibility that I impressed him with my skills as a cop," he said, "I'm inclined to agree. He knew about all my better moments; gave them to me chapter and verse. Flattering as all hell." The cigar-end traced an incendiary circle in the dark, like a July 4th sparkler. "I gotta say I didn't put any store in that old 'innocent man' stall; I wanted to tag along with you to make sure a good verdict didn't go down the drain on account of a road-show Robin Hood like you: You said it yourself when I threw in. Now the situation's starting to stink like this shithole. Got an opinion?"

"Take the job."

"I thought you'd say that, now that I know what to expect. So now I'm a double agent. You know what happens to them."

"You're a grown man, Kopernick. But assuming you survive, I'd owe you one."

He stabbed out the stogie against a leathery palm; an old G.I. trick, but not exclusive to the military. I'd used it myself, when I was too scared to show fear. After all this time the scars look like liver spots.

He got up, extricating himself from a chair with worn-out springs, as smoothly as a camel rising from its knees; no grunts, no cracking of bones, and without using the arms for support. I envied that, but it surprised me less than when he closed the distance between us and stuck out a paw the size of a dinner plate. I was two blocks gone before I could feel my fingers.

EIGHTEEN

'd tied the Gordian knot trying to find the house on Hastings. Now I had to think upside down and backwards just to get loose. It wasn't all bad; by the time I came to a block that looked familiar I was convinced I'd lost any tail I might have picked up. All the headlights in the rearview mirror either fell too far behind to maintain practical surveillance or turned off the street.

I didn't know if the party I'd first spotted in my building, and again from my car across the street, even had a vehicle, or if the whole thing was just a byproduct of my overdeveloped sense of awareness. It's one of the pitfalls of the profession, as potentially dangerous as no awareness at all.

But looking for shadows distracted me from turning over the conversation with Kopernick in my head, and that was a good thing. The more I dwelt on it, the less certain I'd be that: (1) he was just leading me on, letting me think our alliance was genuine to give him more time to scheme with his new employer, or (2) he was on the square, and he had some sense of justice after all. One way seemed like I was too suspicious to recognize a break when it came along, the other like after all these years in the cockpit I was still as green as I was at the start.

It was enough to make me wish I actually had a stalker to keep me occupied.

In any case I was too keyed up to go home, so I made a detour downtown.

I'd left the office before the mail ran. Maybe Publishers Clearing House had come through for me with a thick juicy steak of a check and I could retire to a less miserable climate—the Aleutians, maybe—and a daily pastime that didn't involve sorting out the lies from the half-truths, treading the high-wire between the crooks who wanted me dead and the cops who wanted me incarcerated, and murky conferences after dark in shells of houses that smelled like rodent musk and cheap cigars.

The atmosphere in my little reception room wasn't much of an improvement. The building's cleaning service bought its dusting spray in industrial drums; I kept expecting to see the company's name on a TV pitch to join a class-action suit for some corrosive disease. Under that was the stale stench of no one getting rich anytime this century either. The small scatter of envelopes under the mail slot in the private office confirmed that: Most of them read THIRD NOTICE. I picked them up, carried them to the desk, and started to file them under the blotting pad with the others. The desk lamp was off and the ambient light coming through the window from streetlamps, neighboring buildings, and traffic two stories down made the shadows in the corners as thick as syrup.

I didn't get as far as the blotter. A window in a dark room makes an excellent mirror, reflecting a long plank of face with a moustache like an inverted horseshoe. I twisted away from the glass, dropped the mail, and swept up the Magnum, all in the same movement. The owner of the reflection was harder to see in person, but I saw a flash of movement and fired at the thickest part of his body; just fast enough to deflect his own aim. Instead of my head, something hard and heavy struck the big muscle on the side of my neck. Orange and purple light lanced my vision. I staggered, grabbed for the edge of the desk, got it, found focus, and raised the gun again; but there was nothing to shoot at but the wall opposite. I was alone in the room.

The desk was much bigger than I remembered. Reaching across it with my vision dazzled by the revolver flare and the blow and my ears ringing from the echo of the blast, was like crawling home through a fog so thick it made a hundred yards seem like a mile. At length my hand found the base of the lamp, climbed the flexible post to the switch, and twisted it on. I blinked away the tears, and when my pupils caught up with the light I wobbled across to the open door, and across the reception room to the hallway. There I did the policeman's waltz, pirouetting right and left with the Ruger clasped in both hands.

I was still alone, of course. I was too late even to hear feet hammering the stairs and the street door slamming shut; if a man fleeing the scene of a crime ever bothered with that courtesy.

Holstering the weapon, I started back toward the office, saw a chain of dark spots on the floor. They might have been a trick of shadow. I retreated a step and flipped up the wall switch. In the light from the ceiling fixture, they were glistening red; four pea-size specks leading toward the hallway. I went out there and found six more between the door and the stairs. My sharpshooting skills weren't as bad as I'd feared; I could still hit a target the size of a man at a distance of three feet.

The Easter eggs continued to come. Re-entering the office, my foot nudged something lying on the threshold. I bent and picked it up: a black nylon gauntlet studded with tiny steel ball bearings. A sap glove. Almost no one ever bothers to put one on; just slapping it across someone's temple is enough to bring on concussion. It was pure luck I'd moved in time to deflect his aim.

Not that my neck would thank me. The muscle felt hot and big, and it throbbed. I touched it. I wouldn't make that mistake again. I had to snatch hold of the door frame to stay off the floor.

I was sweating like a victim of yellow fever. I reached up to swipe my forehead, stopped short of knocking myself out cold; the hand was the one holding the mail glove.

Leaning against the jamb, I looked at the object with new eyes. It's a restricted item, like machine guns, blackjacks, and brass knuckles. A private citizen can't obtain any of them without going through the black market, and the paper trail is hard to avoid, even in our paperless society. Most civilians don't bother. Only a cop can carry one around without raising suspicion.

NINETEEN

T hat's the theory," John Alderdyce said, "but a theory is all
it is. These days you can order a Sherman tank online, and
unless some government spook stumbles on the transac-
tion while it's in progress, you'll waste less time later digging up
Jimmy Hoffa."

The inspector stood in the middle of my office, counting the
fingers on the heavy glove over and over. His dress was more
casual than usual: open-necked shirt, gabardine jacket, gray flan-
nels, loafers with tassels. I'd called him at home.

I didn't respond. The face I'd seen reflected in the window belonged to the man I'd spotted twice on my coattails. If Kopernick
had lied about tacking him to me—playing both ends against the
middle, just as he'd said he was doing with Chester Goss—I didn't
want Alderdyce to know just yet we'd agreed to work together.
Trusting just one cop at a time was more than my share of risk.

I said, "He'd been through my desk and my file drawers. I'm
not OCD, but I know when things have been rearranged and when
a drawer I'd shut is left open half an inch. Nothing missing, based
on the first pass-through. Anyway I don't transcribe my notes to
a typewritten file until I close a case or it closes me. If he's interested in an old investigation, I wouldn't know where to start. All I
know is I might as well have stuck with my old lock."

"Even if anyone ever bothered to pull on a sapper," he said, "he'd have taken it off to thumb through the files. So we've got a souvenir, anyway—evidence, on the off chance he left behind a traceable amount of DNA and he's in the database. He probably thought it would be as easy as checking your computer. *Mazel tov!* Took you thirty years to show a profit for staying stuck in the Stone Age."

"Patience is a virtue." My neck felt stiff and swollen, but the throbbing had faded to a dull timpani. It hurt to swallow; but then again I wasn't stretched out in Detroit Receiving Hospital being fed through a tube. "What about the bloodstains? I didn't look past the stairs."

"I didn't see any there, or on the sidewalk. He wasn't hit so bad he couldn't staunch the bleeding with a hand or a handkerchief on the run." Once again he fingered the base of the slug in the wall opposite the desk; it had buried itself there after grazing its victim. "*How* close did you say he was when you shot him?"

"Go ahead, ride me. It was dark and we were both moving. Next time a paper silhouette on the police range jumps you from three feet away, let me know how you did."

"Don't get all pouty," he said. "You're lucky I don't clip you for that unregistered cannon. Forensics is on its way. We'll test the blood and the glove. Might have results by Memorial Day. Meanwhile you know where we're headed."

I was tired and sore. Making a face took no effort. "I hear most of the departments have transferred the mugs from those big smelly books to a computer file: Scroll through 'em fast and be done by lunch."

"I heard that too. Better grab a bite now."

The same eager young cop who'd printed me after the bank shooting—was it still the same week?—entered the interview room carrying a stack of atlas-size books, steadying it with his chin. He bumped the door shut with his hip and dumped his load on the table where I was sitting. Essence of Mummy puffed out from between pages and laid a fresh stratum on top of the tobacco in my lungs. I coughed into the crook of my elbow and asked him how far these things went back.

"I couldn't guess," he said. "We don't date them, like yearbooks."

"I only ask because I think one of these mug shots is Killer Burke. He's been dead since 1940."

The vapid smile I got said he'd had no idea the calendar went back that far. When he left, I slid the top tome off the heap and opened it to another album of known ne'er-do-wells.

Most ran pretty much to a type, except for the eyes. They were as many and as various as species of marine life: narrow-gauge and spread wide, hard as rivets and empty as holes in a bowling ball, pupils shrunken to invisibility, pupils so swollen they erased the irises; eyes burning so hot with hate it was like staring directly at the sun, eyes as cold as permafrost; animal eyes, wild eyes, calculating eyes, ravenous eyes, eyes bloated with sin, eyes disconnected from anything that resembled a brain; every now and then, say on one page in five, eyes so frankly astonished to find themselves staring into a police lens you were sure the owner had been railroaded by an uncaring system; and those were the most dangerous of all.

I thumped another book shut, sat back, and rubbed my own eyes. By now they would look as bad as the worst in the gallery.

My watch read either 12:10 or 2:00 A.M.; the face swam. Whichever it was, I'd pondered weak and weary over too many a quaint and curious volume of forgotten crime for one night. I stood, stretched, cracked my joints, peeled my shirt away from my back, and wandered out into the half-empty squad room.

Alderdyce had gone home; after all, it wasn't *his* office the lab rats were turning inside-out. Compared to mine at that moment, Detroit Homicide was a mortuary. A plainclothesman in shirtsleeves and a shoulder rig lounged in a Staples chair with a stockinged foot perched on an open desk drawer, murmuring into a cell. An Adam-and-Eve team, a female detective and a male, sat opposite each other in joined desks, typing on keyboards connected to bulbous white computer consoles left over from *All the President's Men*. Voices trickled from a loudspeaker mounted on a wall, paying no more attention to what they were saying than anyone on the receiving end. Nothing stirred, not even the dust.

A carafe gurgled on a hot plate. A hand-lettered sign fashioned into a tent told me, with three exclamation points, that the coffee wasn't free; this wasn't a car dealership. I tossed six bits into the tray and waited for it to finish brewing. Pouring took time. The black stuff glorp-glorped into a paper cup with folding handles and from there down my throat, cauterizing the walls still scratchy from the latest assault on my person. I wondered how many that made.

My guy wouldn't be in any of the books. He wasn't local. I couldn't take that into a courtroom, but I was as sure of it as I was that a routine sweep of the clinics, hospitals, and doctors' offices in the metropolitan area wouldn't turn up a man being treated for a gunshot wound. At least not that man. He hadn't bled enough, and no bullet needed extracting. Any first-aid kit would do the job.

Dick Tracy, Jr. came through as I was dropping the cup of medical waste into a lined trash can. He was schlepping another pile of literature. He didn't see me standing there. I left as he was fumbling open the door to the interview room with a free finger. No one tackled me on the way out.

Pausing on the front step to light a cigarette, I admired our false dawn: The lights of the city reflected on the belly of the overcast. It was cold silver, contributing to the raw cold of the vernal equinox. Something black fluttered once around the lighted globe with

POLICE stenciled on it and vanished into the icy mist; a rogue bat, too eager for prey to stick out hibernation. I wondered if it had an investigator's license.

A pair of headlights swept around the corner, plowing my way, eerily without noise, as if it were being towed by the twin beams crawling with vapor. I dropped the cigarette and leaped back into the shelter of the doorway, reaching for the Magnum I wasn't wearing now; an up-to-date carry permit doesn't swing any weight in the cop house.

The car stopped as silently as it had approached. A window slid down, but no gun barrel came poking out through the opening, just a narrow face with a wide mouth, pleats in the cheeks, and gray eyes with no more expression in them than circles punched from cardboard.

"I can see you," Chester Goss said. "That camouflage outfit only works in the dark."

I stepped forward. "This can't be coincidence. It can't survive within a hundred yards of a police precinct. You got the place bugged or what?"

"You don't turn over as many perps as I have without making friends in the department. This is taxpayer property. Anyone who walks in is automatically in public domain. Can I give you a lift?"

"I've got a car."

"Just around the block, then. I feel bad about the way I treated you at my place. Give me a chance to make up for it."

"It's late. I thought all you on-air talents had to get your beauty sleep."

"My studio's downtown. I've been all night editing our annual season-end recap of the cases we worked. It takes me a long time to wind down. You can help." He tilted his head toward the passenger's seat.

I stepped down and around and got in. I was like the bat; too involved in the chase to hang myself upside-down safe at home.

TWENTY

t was a Tesla; that explained the stealth entrance. Sewing machines are louder. It smelled like a new plastic toy, accelerated without a burp, and reached forty by the time we got to the corner.

"Ever drive one of these?" Goss said.

"What do you think?"

He might have chuckled. It made no more noise than the engine. "All you locals think the electric motor's a conspiracy aimed directly at Detroit. I've got a Camaro on lease and sixty thousand invested in the upkeep on a '68 Mustang. Does that let me back in the club?"

"You misunderstand me. I don't care if you've got a Japanese Zero in a private hangar. I was talking about the size of my bank balance."

"Funny."

"What's funny?"

"The timing. But then I'm in a business that runs by the clock, so I'm sensitive to that kind of thing."

I let it go. I had a good idea where he was headed, but it wasn't my place to step on his punchline. Timing's my thing, too.

He was dressed for work behind the camera: slacks from an old suit, deck shoes thinning at the toes, U of D sweatshirt. I pointed at the shirt. "I wouldn't have tagged you for a Catholic."

"I don't fit the mold? Didn't know there was one."

"There isn't. I only see you on the receiving end of the confession box."

"I lapsed."

He turned the corner with one hand on the bottom of the wheel, cruised down an empty street. I ran down my window to listen to the never-ending hum from the freeways. All that silence in the airtight cabin was murder on the nerves.

"Been a long day for me, too," I said. "I started out in prison and wound up thumbing through photo albums in a police interrogation room."

"So my spies tell me." He shook his head. "Wild Bill's got nothing on you. That's two shootings in a week."

"It's been a slow week."

He drummed his fingers on the wheel. "Are you always this hard to start a conversation with?"

"I'm a chatterbox when I'm not dead tired. If you picked me up to hear all about my adventures in the detective trade, I'll have to charge you for the research."

"Idle curiosity. Call it a busman's holiday. You don't turn off the sleuthing after the five o'clock whistle."

"Still waiting for the other shoe," I said.

He swung into a side street, coasted to a stop in front of a row of houses, some of them with the lights on. The morning shift at Ford and Chrysler starts early. A soporific mosquito wobbled into the car and sang in my ear: It sounded like a drunk crooning "Old Man River." My bat wasn't so far ahead of the season after all. I ran up the window.

Goss twisted around to face me, one arm slung across the back of his seat. He looked older in the greenish glow from the dials on the dash. It would take an expert in studio makeup to fill in those trenches under his eyes.

"We got off on the wrong foot before," he said. "Mea culpa.

When you told me you were reopening the case, it was like the last twenty years hadn't happened. That's why I don't keep a lot of pictures of April in my house. Anytime I want to see her, all I have to do is close my eyes."

His voice shook a little. It was important to remember he played to an audience for a living.

"I'm sorry for your loss," I said. "I should have said that the other day."

"That's a police phrase. It must be in the manual. Not that anything more original would help. You got kids, Walker?"

I shook my head. I wanted to smoke, but I didn't want to air the place out and let any more early skeeters into the car.

"You don't know, then. Put short, you're not supposed to outlive your children. It's a crime against nature. And you know how I feel about crime. Which was part of it, how I reacted."

He shifted his attention to the windshield, opaque now with only darkness in front of it. "I'm a salesman," he said. "I peddle justice. If I ran all the stories I covered where a guilty man went free because of an overwrought cop or an incompetent clerk or a bleeding-heart judge, *Dogs* wouldn't last a season. I follow an investigation for weeks, months sometimes, waiting for some animal to get what's coming to him, and when he doesn't—when it looks like he's even better off for what he did—I want to buy a gun and make my own correction in the corrections system. But I don't, because of the thing I've appointed myself to defend. That doesn't make it any easier." He turned back my way. "So maybe you can see how I felt when it looked like you were out to spring that filth that killed my little girl."

"What if he didn't?" I said. "Putting aside the innocent-man-wronged angle, it means the filth that did it is still on the loose."

"Vail told me you said something like that. Yeah, I got it out of her. It wasn't hard. She has no talent for lying. I think that's the reason I was attracted to her in the first place."

He was silent for a moment. Then he shook his head. "I don't buy it, Walker. I couldn't even if I wanted to. I've invested too many years in this thing to cash out now. I won't be one of those grieving cases who say how precious their loved one was to them, when in fact they weren't. April and I didn't get along. I loved her; don't think I didn't, and I think she loved me. But she was always closer to her mother.

"I never even set foot in her apartment," he said. "I didn't approve of her moving out, when she could easily have commuted between school and home. She wasn't mature enough to live on her own. Events proved me right. I wish to God they didn't." He breathed. "Well, there was one thing I could do for her, useless as it was, and I did it. Only now it seems I failed even at that."

A piece of lint on the seat caught his attention. He scraped at it with a nail. It turned out to be part of the upholstery thread. He pressed it back into place, looked at me.

"You're not the weasel I took you for, Walker; I've done my research. I don't get along with the police any better than you do, and we both have to cozy up to crooks to get what we want. I'm sorry I put you in the crossfire."

"I'm not angry, Goss. I've been bounced harder with less reason. If that's not in the P.I. manual, it should be. You didn't have to waste a charge just to square things with me."

"So you're going ahead." It wasn't a question.

I said, "I didn't know April. But if pushing the case against Corbeil was really for her, making sure it really was justice falls into that same category. If not him, it was someone else; and if it was him, taking another hard look at the evidence will nail the thing shut once and for always."

He turned back toward the windshield. His narrow features reflected in the glass belonged to a three-thousand-year-old mummy.

"I don't do my own legwork," he said. "I've hired detectives. I know what they make as independents, because I ask when I interview them for the job. Just doubling the salary would be an insult. I double *that*, and they'll never have to pay for a doctor's appointment again. They don't even see the bill."

I caught myself just short of asking how many expert consultants his show needed; that's how tired I was, ready to tip my hand on my partnership with Kopernick. Instead I said, "What would one of these former investigators do on a TV stage? I'd call dolly grip, but I don't know what that is."

"Chief safety officer: My safety, mostly. I get enough death threats in one week to spook a U.S. president. Most of them come handwritten in crayon. They don't let you have anything sharp in maximum security. Most of them don't amount to anything, but one is all it takes. I need a man who can not only protect me, but turn up a threat and neutralize it before it happens."

"I've done bodyguard work. They never give you anything good to read in places where you sit around on your fanny four hours at a time."

"You'd hire grunts for that. This would be strictly an executive position. Would I employ Al Kaline to serve as equipment manager? The only time you'd carry a weapon would be while you're supervising on the target range. Oh, maybe for show, when I fly to Paris to consult with the Sûreté; London and Scotland Yard. The show's going international next season. Keep that under your hat. We're announcing it at the end of the season recap. First-class flights, the presidential suite in the George V, your own credit line on Savile Row."

When I didn't say anything, he continued. "You can't go on forever staking out strangers' houses and picking up a guy in Royal Oak and following him all the way to Mexico on a diet of burgers and greasy fries." He pointed with his chin. "How long have you been favoring that leg?"

"I don't play favorites." I twisted to face him, dangling my own arm over the back of the seat. "If I took the job—assuming you're offering me a job—could I finish the April Goss case before I start ordering mimosas on the Left Bank?"

"You'll have to leave that to the police; they're interested again, by the way. You did your job. My current head of security's leaving Friday. He wants to spend more time with his grandchildren. Severance package I gave him, he can send them to Harvard. I can't leave my flanks exposed without a backup in place. Insurance companies get snippy when they've got ten million riding on your head."

"Thanks, Goss. Don't lose any sleep over my bum leg. I've got a spare."

"That's a no?"

"I just got English down. I'm too old to start on French, and I wouldn't know how to behave myself in a silk suit. I hear they ride up on your crotch."

"Joking aside," he said.

"Joking aside."

He drummed his fingers again. "Sure? The offer expires with this joyride."

"I'm parked behind the precinct. My leg will thank you if you pull around."

This time the tires chirped when he took off. Back at the Second he swung in behind my Cutlass; of course he knew what I drive. I grasped the door handle, looked over at him. "Don't think I didn't appreciate the vote of confidence."

"I guess I'm not so great a salesman after all. You'd have made a fine department chief."

"That's not the job I'm talking about." I got out.

TWENTY-ONE

How'd you do it?"

It was a new day, but it didn't make me feel any less old. I'd gotten home just in time to catch some dark, but I was too exhausted to sleep, and the weak drink I made only woke me up wider. Something's gone wrong with the universe when liquor lets you down. I'd finally caught a couple of hours, but I'd have been better off, more alert, if I'd just stayed up.

Now I was sitting in the breakfast nook over coffee and toast, talking to Chrys Corbeil on my cell. She'd called just as I was filling my mug, asking me in her low, clear voice how I did it.

"I can't discuss trade secrets," I said. "I can tell you the dove was never in the handkerchief."

"I mean how'd you get Dan to change his mind? He called me last night from Huron Valley to apologize for losing his temper with me and to tell me he agreed to be your client."

"Not me. Michael Mihalich; that's the lawyer who defended him at his trial. I'm still working for you. He's my tin mitts in case the police decide to take me down for withholding evidence. Lawyers can do that, up to a point. I can't. Doesn't mean I don't; but you can't do legwork with chains on your ankles. This way I avoid that."

"Why would Dan agree to engage the lawyer who lost his case?"

"Maybe because it means he'll try harder this time, and with more experience under his belt. But mostly because there's not much else to do in stir but look for a way out, and I talked him out of the first one he had planned."

"You said something about chains on your ankles. What reason would the police have to stop you?"

"None, except with them, stopping people comes naturally. Between us, I think it's unlikely this time: The only active member of the department who was directly involved with the original investigation says he's working with me, and I've decided to take comfort in what he says. But to get back to what you asked, your brother's turned an important corner. He's given up giving up."

"I'm so happy! But—"

I thought I heard a thumb being bitten.

"Yeah, there's that," I said. "Don't think I haven't considered it. If I fumble the ball, he'll be right back where he was. No, he'll be worse off because he let himself hope."

"That makes your job harder, doesn't it?"

"Nothing could make this one harder, but it ratchets up the entertainment value." I gulped coffee, forgetting it was still steaming from the carafe. I made a noise.

"Are you all right?"

I cleared my throat. "Nothing. Until a second ago I forgot I had a little blunt-force trauma to my neck last night." I told her about that.

"My God! Are you all right? What's a sap glove?"

"If I thought that's something you'd ever need to know, I'd use one to clobber myself. I'm okay. A Whac-a-Mole's got nothing on me when it comes to taking hits from the neck up."

"Do you think it had anything to do with what you're doing for Dan?"

"The cops asked me the same thing. The answer is I don't know, but I'm going to proceed as if it did."

"How is that?"

"No idea."

A beetle buzzed in my ear. I looked at the screen. Alderdyce was trying to call. I hit Ignore, munched toast. "There are other developments, which may or may not have any bearing on the job. I'll report about them when I know."

"Thank you, Mr. Walker. You've—oh, you don't know what you've done."

"I usually don't." We said a couple more polite things and were through talking to each other. I was about to punch Call Back when I heard footsteps on the wooden porch.

I'm a connoisseur of footsteps. Two hundred ten pounds of department brass ought to have punched holes in the boards, but this one took his cue from the elephant; its tons leave shallow tracks, treading lightly and testing the ground as it goes.

I dusted the crumbs off my shirt and got up to answer his knock.

"'Morning, Inspector. Nice of you to drop in. Why bother to call when you were on the way already?"

John Alderdyce crossed the threshold in a steel-gray double-breasted with a splash of yellow at his throat. He shut the door behind him and lowered himself into the overstuffed chair, unbuttoning his coat in the same movement.

"I couldn't get you at the office," he said. "You'd think this was a hobby, the hours you keep. But like you said, I was on my way."

I didn't press it. He was under the impression his physical presence was more intimidating than his voice on the phone. He was wrong. He could be just as formidable by carrier pigeon.

"Coffee? I made a big pot."

"I gave it up. It keeps me awake nights, just like you. You stole out from the Second without saying good-bye. You hurt Officer Cochran's feelings. There he was, standing in an empty room with a stack of mug books and a silly look on his face."

I sat on the couch between the broken spring and the Bermuda Triangle in the middle.

"So that's his name," I said. "My guy's not in there, John. Whoever put him on me wouldn't use anyone local. He's too cagy to risk my recognizing his guy."

"To know that, you'd have to know who it was put him on to you."

"At this point it's just a guess. I'll tell you when it's more."

"Tell me, or Stan Kopernick?"

I didn't ask how he'd found out we were working together. I knew enough about Alderdyce not to be curious. "Who'd I call after I saw my visitor out of the office?"

"Who you call when you just got jumped isn't the same thing as who you call when you turned up the right rock and saw what was under it. This is still a police case, Walker. They're never really closed, just like no volcano's ever really extinct."

I excused myself to go to my bedroom closet and came back with lawyer Mihalich's card from my suitcoat pocket. "Ask him. I doubt he'll give you much. He's my client. You know what that means."

He looked at the card and slapped it down on an oaken post of thigh. "Just how many clients do you have on this one case, and is that ethical? Look who I'm asking."

"It is when all their interests coincide. I'm only being paid by one, if you don't count the buck I got from Mihalich. I looked it up in the penal code." I grinned. "Ain't the law grand?"

"I wouldn't know. I don't understand it. I only enforce it—when it lets me."

I got it that I was supposed to feel sorry for him. I threw him a bone.

"I'm not supposed to recognize the party who gave it to me in the neck, but I've seen him somewhere before he wandered into my building the first time; I thought that then and I know it now. Can't quite finger him, but it wasn't in person and it wasn't in a mug shot."

"That's specific."

"It's as close as I can come. Chances are I'll remember where it was and under what circumstances when I'm thinking about something else. That's a challenge at the moment."

He picked up the business card, stretching it between his fingers like Silly Putty. The fingers were long and tapering, more like a pianist's than a cop who'd served his time in the trenches with a nightstick. He scaled it onto the coffee table between us. "So where do you go from here? I'm not expecting a straight answer. I have to go through the motions or the city won't pay."

"Weighing my options." I weighed one right then; decided to use it. "Chester Goss offered me a bribe last night."

When he frowned he looked like a Tiki god. I saw black clouds gathering. Then they parted. He turned up a palm. "Not even a misdemeanor. You're not a public servant."

"Aren't you the least bit interested why?"

"I *know* why. I've seen his show. If this town had a bat signal he'd spend all his nights looking out the window. He treats every violent crime like a personal insult. When it *is* personal, like say his daughter's murder, I wouldn't put it past him to offer a Supreme Court justice a month in Bermuda with hot-and cold-running wahins to get what he wants."

"I don't think they have wahins in Bermuda."

"Like I'd get the chance to find out for myself. What's the going rate now for an over-the-hill P.I. with the bit in his teeth?"

"A Paris suite, champagne on takeoff, and a dental plan. For that bit in my teeth," I added.

"If I were you, I'd take it." He looked around the room. "Maybe you could afford to hire a decorator. This dump has all the charm of a monastery."

"It's just a place to change horses. He made the same pitch to Kopernick, Goss did. One like it."

"Him I wouldn't have to advise. He's probably out shopping for a beret right now."

"He says he's just stringing Goss along. Could be I'm on the same string." I rolled a shoulder. "I wish I could tag that guy. Just when I think I can trust him not to be trusted, he flips over and shows me his belly. Once a cop's bent he should stay that way."

"Now I think of it," Alderdyce said, "I don't see him bought, not with money. Put down an unarmed suspect, then plant a throw-away on him, yeah; pinch an apple off a street cart, maybe. Meet a guy on Belle Isle at midnight with a suitcase full of cash, no." He frowned again, shook his head. "No. Cop with his seniority has had plenty of opportunities to flip off his pension and retire early. This one time he might be on the up-and-up."

"Bummer. Hating him was simple. Just disliking him's going to take work."

The phone rang next to the armchair. I got up and lifted the receiver, listened to the voice on the other end, cupped my hand over the mouthpiece. "A minute, John? The Phoenix Cremation Service wants to give me a sweetheart deal."

"Sure." He stood, all of a piece, without bracing his hands on the arms. His big bony head just cleared the ceiling. "Don't tell him what I said about the throwaway piece. I may have to work with him myself someday."

Alderdyce's built-in smoke detector was dead-on. Kopernick announced himself with his trademark, clearing twenty years of cigar exhaust from his throat. I snatched away the receiver, a half-second too late to avoid bruising my eardrum.

"Something," he said.

"I heard it. You ought to give up smoking old tires."

"Tell it to the Surgeon General. It ain't evidence, but I learned a long time ago to pay attention when my gut starts barking."

"Pepto-Bismol."

"You gonna keep dicking around or what? Meet me."

I cleared my throat in a positive response. I didn't have to ask where. I made the necessary arrangements and made sure I had no company when I left, from either side of the law.

Hastings—the obstructed bowel that was left of it—didn't look any less dismal in daylight; more so, in fact. A ground mist made up entirely of its murky past hung at windowsill height above the jungle of urban alfalfa, forty-ounce empties, and car batteries. The asbestos tile was dingy with yellow jaundice. When I slammed my door, a startled pheasant exploded out the broken window with a noise like an outboard motor, cackling as it wheeled into the sun. A city of vacant lots makes a swell game preserve.

This time I'd prepared myself better, shaking the dead spiders out of a pair of insulated boots and lacing them up to my knees. Whatever had bitten me on my last visit had left a red welt on the ankle that burned like brand-new when I put alcohol on it. The boots pinched my feet; pounding a few thousand miles of pavement had spread them out since my hunting days. Nevertheless I went for the land-speed record sprinting across the shaggy lawn.

The door was bolted this time, and I didn't like that any more than when I'd found it unlocked before.

I unholstered the .38 and rapped the stump of muzzle against a panel. The heavy-duty Ruger was for formal wear after six o'clock.

A throat got cleared on the other side. It sounded like a log collapsing in a fireplace grate. "Walker?"

"Room service."

Boards shifted. Metal grated against metal, the door opened, and a blue steel barrel poked through a space the width of the detective's face; which was wide enough to let out another pheasant if there was a colony inside.

No pheasant came out. What did was less welcome: an acrid stench that would be with me for the rest of the day, like a tune I couldn't shake and had never liked in the first place.

TWENTY-TWO

Kopernick tilted the pistol upward, one hand gripping the opposite wrist in the approved manner. It was a SIG Sauer; you couldn't miss the no-nonsense L-shape of the Budweiser of police sidearms. His mud-colored eyes looked past my shoulder, slid right and left the length of the stubby street. He lowered the hammer and stepped away from the door. I put up the .38, pushed in, and kicked the door shut.

Inside, the smell was overpowering. It might have been Riverside Park just after the Independence Day fireworks.

By day the room was no cozier than it had seemed at night. If anything, the smudgy light seeping in through the one unboarded window exposed it for what it was: the shell of something that hadn't offered much promise in the beginning. A burst sofa sagged against a papered wall broken up by dark squares where pictures had hung. The oil lamp Kopernick had lit the night before stood on an end table with duct tape binding three of its four legs, next to the armchair, which even he might not have sat on had he seen it clearly; that was it for furniture. In that setting—a place where some family had survived until it didn't anymore—the thing heaped on the floor among shards of fallen plaster, rodent droppings, and a mountain of dirty pink insulation from the fallen-in ceiling might have been part of the decorating scheme. It looked like just a pile of clothes, except for the shoes. They only land on their heels when the feet are still inside them.

"How many notches does this make?" I said.

"Go to hell."

His tone was shallow, as if he was breathing through his mouth to avoid the stink of burnt cordite. It drew my attention away from the corpse. His face had a greenish cast. I'd seen that before, in the mirror the first time I'd shot to kill. You never know about people. Maybe it affected him that way every time.

I looked again at the body. It wore a gray hoodie that the last time it was washed might have been blue, jeans fraying through at the ankles, where the knobby bone gnawed at the cloth, filthy sneakers. The face was turned from me, a cheek resting on the floor. Clenching my jaws, I stooped, gathered a handful of jersey cloth, and pulled. The neck offered no resistance. With the dead man staring at the ceiling—through it, actually, all the way to forever—I looked at a plank of face so pale it made the inverted-horseshoe moustache look like a spill of fresh tar.

Bloody torn fabric traced a diagonal line across the front of the hoodie, just below the strings designed to close the hood. It looked like a continuous gash, but was probably three holes grouped within an inch of one another. Virgin or not, Kopernick had the training and the coolness under pressure of a man born to the blue.

"I didn't know him from Bigfoot," he said. "You?"

"Not to speak to. He's been in my hip pocket for a couple days. Oh, and I shot him; I should've mentioned that."

"I heard you shot somebody. Sure it's him?"

Time to clench again. I took hold of the sweatshirt lower down and jerked it up above his navel. A square of gauze was taped to his ribs on the right side. He'd bled through it, but not much. The stain was yellowish.

I straightened. "I discouraged him, I guess. Anyway he switched targets."

"I never spotted him. I thought he was you; stood here with my thumb up my ass and let him walk right in. Drew down on me with that." He was still holding his pistol. He pointed it at a short-barreled revolver lying in a corner out of the corpse's reach. It had a dull black finish and rubber bands wound around the grips. In Detroit you can get a Saturday Night Special any day of the week. Still, he'd upgraded his choice of weapons; if he'd had it with him when he was tossing my office, he wouldn't have bothered with a sap glove.

Kopernick said, "I kicked it out of his hand when he dropped. Let some lab monkey do the picking up. That's one less hour I'll spend with the review board."

I bent over the stiff again. Not to check vitals; one look at his face told me he was all through with those. "Wish I could place him," I said. "Not anyone I met in person; at least not before this week. Some stranger at a party."

"You're not too picky about who you hang out with." He slid the Sig into his belt clip. "He was gonna use that popgun on me. Why, I don't ask. No limit these days on how many cops you bag. I liked him better when it looked random. Think he was self-employed or on somebody else's clock?"

"He was new at it either way. Anyone with experience would've armed himself better. Call it in?"

"Not yet. I need a story. I'm not officially on this beef. Officially there *is* no beef. I already took it on the ear for being off the reservation when the shit flew. That time I *saved* a life. It won't go down so good this time."

"Give it to Alderdyce. He knows the rest of it, and he's in a position to sell it downtown. I didn't tell him," I said, when he looked at me. "The plumbing's full of holes. You said it yourself."

"You gonna hang around?"

"I don't know what I could add, apart from more paperwork. You're already out of the running for Employee of the Month."

The face under the hat brim darkened; but he slid a phone from an inside pocket.

I held up a hand. "First, what brought me down here? Not just to hear your side of the shoot. He's still too fresh for that."

He put away the phone, but kept his hand inside his coat. "Something you said last time we were here made me think of it."

I gave him my best blank look; best meaning it was genuine.

He reached deeper under the coat and took out something bulky. I'd thought he'd looked a little more well-stuffed than usual.

When someone sticks something at you, taking it is almost automatic; a quirk of human nature. The last time I did that, I woke up in Detroit Receiving with steel pins in one of my ribs. I kept my hands at my sides. Not that the thing looked so sinister: It was a common hand towel in a fold, white with a green stripe at each end.

He shook it, daring me to take it. I gave in then. The towel smelled stale and didn't feel crisp from the laundry, but then it had been plastered against Stan Kopernick's abdomen for nobody but he knew how long.

"I won't say where I got it," he said. "Not yet. Funny, considering what I think of them lab monkeys, I should be the one to wonder what a fresh look at a twenty-year-old case might turn up."

It dawned slowly, like a blossom opening in stop-motion. I said, "Why me? Give it to Alderdyce too."

"I was going to, after I showed it to you, partner. Now it just might get lost in the shuffle. If I'm right, that rag and this rack of ribs here belong to the same party." He grinned his shark's grin. "I got the idea mucking around them files in the basement at the Second."

He dialed the Second Precinct and asked for the inspector. Waiting, he fired up a cigar; it was an even bet which reek came out on top. I let myself out.

I pitched the towel onto the passenger's seat and cranked the starter. I had everything I needed now. All I had to do was prove it.

TWENTY-THREE

Look who's here," Barry said. "I knew you couldn't pass up the Tuesday tapeworm special at Carver's."

For once I wasn't up to it. "I need access to your cloud, or whatever it is you call it." I told him what I was after and what I'd been up to. It didn't take as long as I thought.

"I can't leave you alone for a minute," he said. "Yeah, I've got it; also *Cops, America's Most Wanted, 60 Minutes, 48 Hours, Crime 360,* and two hours to kill before my tea with Frankie 'Big Neck' Siciliano. Step into my parlor." He slid away from the door.

He was in his back-to-basics period, sub-leasing a condo on the ground floor of a building where they used to build Liberty ships on the Short Cut Channel of the River Rouge. The current owner had whitewashed the bricks and replaced the big gridded windows with solar panels, but there was still a slight tinge of soldering compound in the air. That part might have been just my imagination; it would be a week before my nasal membranes recovered from *eau de* O.K. Corral. I followed him into a combination living room/office/sleeping chamber big enough to dry-dock a destroyer, with exposed overhead pipes and steel beams painted a neutral shade that made them recede into the fifteen-foot ceiling. The décor, eighties duck-and-basket, screamed previous tenant; decades after Barry had turned an ignition key and blown a quarter of his anatomy to smithereens, he still lived on the principle that nothing he owned couldn't be left behind on three minutes' notice.

Six sticks of dynamite ought to have cut in half his trip to Paradise, but some amateur had taped them to the heat shield instead of under the hood. Barry owed his life to Detroit steel.

I looked around with my hands in my pockets. A tin reproduction of an old-fashioned sign advertising overalls read WEARS LIKE A PIG'S SNOUT. "How do you stand it?"

"The roof don't leak and I've got a honey of a view of Zug Island." He sat down on a rocking chair in front of a rustic table and swept the screen saver off a desktop computer; this season it was a cheesecake photo of Virginia Hill, Bugsy Siegel's squeeze. "Pull up an orange crate," he said.

The choice wasn't much better than that. I slid a sling-back thing of canvas and bleached maple up to a corner of the table.

His fingers were a blur on the keyboard. The screen scrambled and a hellish mix of electric guitars, electronic synthesizers, and French horns burst from the pocket-size speakers. He ran down the volume until the ceiling beams stopped vibrating. Grainy, jagged black-and-white images stuttered across the monitor at opposing angles, a disorienting effect: SWAT teams boiling into action, fugitives in flight, suspects slung across fenders and cuffed, cars in hot pursuit; the seamy life as seen through a detached retina. A thud, as of a steel door slamming shut, followed by a close-up of a CGI-enhanced Doberman, red-eyed and foaming at the mouth, and ragged blood-red letters making a gory slash across the screen:

CUTTHROAT DOGS

Snarling, the dog seized the legend in its jaws and shook it to pieces. Then the image dissolved into a close-up of a stern, vertically pleated face. Superimposed on this, in simple block characters, orderly and reassuring:

Your Host
Chester Goss

Barry waited, fingers hovering above the keyboard.

I said, "I need to surf through every episode going back five years."

"That's *all*?"

"To start."

"Frankie Big Neck might spot me fifteen minutes, but not twelve hours."

"Goss runs a recap at the end of each season. That help?"

"I wish you'd said that in the first place. I was kidding about the fifteen minutes. He'd squiff me after five." He pressed a key, brought up a grid that looked like a menu from a Chinese restaurant, scrolled down Column A, found what he wanted, tickled another key. When the orange came back on, he fast-forwarded to Goss's face—just as stern, but less pleated by five years—paused on a subhead reading THE YEAR IN REVIEW, then proceeded through the episode, first jumping ahead chapter by chapter, then slowing to frame by frame when I called out, on to the acknowledgments at the end of the entry; a longer list than usual, crediting all the officers and agencies who'd cooperated over the past season. I made a rolling gesture with my hands and we sped to the recap for the next year.

We kept at it for an hour and a half, freeze-framing from time to time on a face that looked promising, then whizzing forward. At the end of each episode, a number appeared, each numeral sliding into place as on a digital alarm clock, reporting the latest tally of felons brought to justice as a result of information volunteered by viewers reporting the whereabouts of featured criminals. Even allowing for the flimsiest connection to the material provided by the show, the total was impressive.

Chester Goss had hit on the formula for success when it came to crime coverage: Every day, the media furnished a bounty of atrocities, and averaged only a handful of arrests and convictions per month. *Cutthroat Dogs* reported a nearly 100 percent record of cases closed, and closed for good. It didn't matter that his staff would select its cases based on the likelihood of imminent apprehensions; a punchy narrative style, rapid-fire editing, and a dramatic musical score kept the audience riveted, with no time to stop and consider the realities or appreciate the meticulous, relentlessly patient process of tracking fugitives, placing them under restraint, and assembling a case that would satisfy first a prosecuting attorney, then a judge, then a jury—all comprised of error-prone humans—and eventually a penal system built on shifting shale. Success at snail's-pace didn't win ratings.

"What a guy!" said Barry, pausing to work the cramps out of his fingers. "Sherlock Holmes, Eliot Ness, J. Edgar, and McGruff the Crime Dog all rolled into one. Shows what any of 'em could've done if they'd just had a smart producer. Notice how there's never any mention of the appeals system? I bet half these mooks either walked or ratted out their friends for eighteen months of community service."

"He said he peddles justice for a living. One unsolved investigation and he's back behind the cutting desk in Southfield." I lit a cigarette off the butt of the last. "Ready when you are, B.S."

"Watch your mouth. What makes you think your guy'll show up?"

"He's like an itch I can't reach. I was wrong in thinking we'd met face-to-face, or even across a busy street. I didn't know that for sure until just a little while ago. I've got Stan Kopernick to thank for that."

"Seems to me last time was for a sock on the jaw."

"You know what they say about last year's enemy. How's your carpal tunnel, all better?"

We were less than halfway through the third season-ender when I leaned forward fast, releasing a shower of sparks onto my shirt. I brushed them off, not quickly enough to avoid burning a hole in the pocket. "Go back!"

He reversed the footage. When I told him to stop, he froze on a narrow face captured from above, staring into a ceiling-mounted surveillance camera. It had no moustache, but it belonged to the man I'd spotted in my building and on the street and finally the slab of meat on the floor of the house on Hastings. It was stamped with the time and date from the original airing. I had Barry go back to the beginning of the segment and play it at normal speed.

The man's name was Kenneth Whitelaw. As summarized by Chester Goss in his trademark hypnotic monotone, two notes deeper than his normal speaking voice, the Georgia native had an arrest record going back to age fourteen, including aggravated assault, armed robbery, breaking and entering, and attempted murder. All but one of the charges had been withdrawn; the assault and murder attempt when the witnesses refused to cooperate with authorities and the armed robbery because the judge who'd authorized the search warrant that had recovered the stolen property from his home had omitted an important piece of punctuation from the language. The B-and-E stuck; his face in the security footage was impossible to challenge, and he was sentenced to thirty-six months in the Georgia state penitentiary at Atlanta.

"I saw this episode," I said, "or maybe the one that broke the story. I didn't remember the details, but certain facial types stay with me. According to this he should still be inside."

Barry snorted. Not many can pull off a snort the way he can. "Reversed on appeal. Good behavior. Escape, possibly. Mistaken identity?"

"Not unless he's twins."

"Unlikely coincidence. Keep going? Goss might have followed up."

"Not in the case of a crook getting released back into the population. He told me himself he wouldn't still be on the air if he couldn't deliver punishment every week."

"'Reality programming.'" Air quotes. He tapped his mouse. Whitelaw disappeared and Virginia returned. Barry sat back. "What tripped your breaker? It's been five years since this guy got into showbiz."

"Kopernick." I told him about the towel. Barry's forehead wrinkled as far as the plate in his skull.

"When did *he* discover science? Last I knew he was a confirmed witch-burner."

"That's probably why he gave it to me. Who'd take it seriously, coming from him?"

"He didn't tell you where he got it?"

"He probably wants me to confirm it first. Two mistakes less than a year apart don't get you a parking spot next to the precinct entrance; he told me so himself. Anyway, I know where he got it. It's Goss's."

TWENTY-FOUR

Barry looked at his watch. His appointment time was coming up. He kept his seat.

I said, "That's not for broadcast. Not yet."

He swiveled a shoulder; made a beckoning gesture with his fingers.

"I saw it when I dropped in on Goss at his house. He was swatting a virtual ball back and forth with a virtual opponent and sweating real sweat. It might not be the same one, but he's the kind of guy whose towels would all match. Did I mention it's a nice house?"

"You know what you're saying?"

"Uh-huh. Chester and April didn't get on like in a Father's Day card. I got that straight from him. He was the kind of family patriarch who didn't like his kid moving out from under his roof—meaning his influence. He said he never even saw her apartment."

"My sister and our dad weren't greeting-card material either," he said. "He threw her out when she was sixteen; I don't know why he didn't do it a lot sooner. It's still a long way from there to murdering your own daughter and framing her boyfriend."

"It *would* go a long way toward explaining why he tried to hire Kopernick and me off the investigation. I don't know what the half-life is on vengeance; twenty years seems like plenty. But not enough to beat a rap that has no statute of limitations."

"If he lied about not visiting her apartment, his DNA would prove it. It wasn't a factor then, but the physical evidence should still be in storage: her clothes, the razor that slit her wrists; hair and skin cells on any surface the team collected. There's only one hitch."

I nodded. "Chain of evidence. Kopernick's word alone about where he got it couldn't swing a court order to force Goss to provide a sample for comparison. As ironclad a case as the prosecution had against O. J., it fell apart because the state couldn't prove the material hadn't been tampered with. But the towel doesn't have to be evidence."

I leaned forward in the sling chair. "Kopernick snitched it, probably when he went to Goss's place to tell him what to do with his job offer. That's a guess, his excuse for being there. He knows I wouldn't buy his going there to beg more time to think about it than he already had. That would only tip off our mark. He got the idea from me, when I told him that Goss had had his ancestry checked.

"Goss may not know it," I said, "but that means his DNA's in the FBI database. This *Roots* kick everyone's on is the best thing that's happened to the feds since the invention of the wiretap."

"I can't imagine he doesn't know. You saw his credit sequence. He has more technical experts on his staff than Quantico."

"He got careless. If he hadn't wanted to set a friendly tone when I came to ask him about the investigation into his daughter's murder, he wouldn't have been so anxious to explain why a grown man would play a foreign sport in the privacy of his study. I called him on it. Being a smart aleck can pay off sometimes, even when you're not trying."

"How much hate does a man have to harbor to make him kill his own offspring?"

"More than what he told me." My turn to shake my head. "It's a screwy theory. The longer I look at it the more holes spring up.

But I can't throw it out till I get that towel tested and get the cops to compare the results to the stuff from the crime scene. Know anybody who conducts genetics experiments out of the trunk of his car?"

He ran his thumb along his space bar; studying the operation as if he were bottling nitroglycerine. I couldn't tell if he'd heard me. "This used to be so simple: Go after the bastards that think the law doesn't apply to them and get them to nail themselves to the cross with their own words; chalk up another win against the blowtorch boys and then on to the next ballpark. Someone got killed, it wasn't any more personal than a house call from the doctor. How'd we get from that to this?"

I said nothing to that. He wasn't expecting an answer.

"Never mind, Barry. I'll find someone. It's a cottage industry. Anything shakes down, you'll get it right after the cops."

"Forget it. I'm retiring."

I drew smoke into my lungs, let it out with a chuckle. "You can't stand up Big Neck. He'll write nasty things about you in his diary."

"Not kidding. I've been thinking about it all year. No, longer; since Congress passed RICO. Who needs an amateur gangbuster if they're willing to burn the Constitution to put a loan shark on liquid oxygen behind bars?"

"Hell with that. John Alderdyce retired, and what's he doing now? Pounding the same old beat."

"He's a cop. It's a medical condition. It's more than just the pointlessness of the whole thing. I'm sick of rotten coffee and stale sandwiches. I want to see what it's like to wake up every morning without wondering who I'm pretending to be today just to root up another crummy lead with my snout. Go a whole week without logging on to find out who's scooping me now, how he did it, and what I need to do to keep it from happening again."

He swiveled my way, tented his shoulders, and let them drop. For the first time I noticed the fissures at the corners of his eyes, the deep trenches from his nostrils to the corners of his mouth. When a party who still looks like Archie and the gang when he's eligible for Medicaid decides to age, he does it all at once.

"Okay," he said, "that's who, how, and what. I'd be tickled pink if the when is tomorrow."

"That's good." I pinched out the butt and dropped it next to the others in a saucer Barry had provided. He'd checked into the hospital a two-pack-a-day smoker and checked out of rehab cold turkey. Three months on your back and six more in physical therapy will change your chemistry. "Off the cuff, or did you scribble it on the palm of your hand? I didn't even see you sneak a peek."

"Go ahead, have your fun. This time next year I plan to be tanning my toes in the tropics."

"You've only got five. How long can that take?"

"That's another thing. What've I got to show after thirty years of meeting people in parking garages and swimming in Dumpsters? An ankle made of pencil lead and a patch to keep my brains from spilling into my hat. You know I've got arthritis in these fingers?" He held up the hand that was missing two. "You'd think I'd be spared at least that in the trade."

"So what? I limp when I'm tired. Two centimeters the other direction and I'd be ashes in a jar. Siegfried—or was it Roy?—got his face eaten by a tiger. Oprah probably has tennis elbow from counting her money. Why now? How come the sudden yen for palm trees and papaya? Just yesterday you were Deadline Dan, Boy Reporter, same as always."

"It's been simmering. Still was yesterday. Yesterday Chester Goss was just a huckster with a gimmick. Today he's a monster who murdered his daughter. Pot's boiling over."

"That's today," I said, "and it's far-fetched. Tomorrow he could be anybody; even somebody who's good enough to share a planet with St. Barry the Unimpeachable." I got up. "Give me a call when you decide the universe is no worse off than it was when you were writing obituaries for the *Free Press*. I'll take you to a joint that specializes in branch water and underbrush."

His jaw dropped into his lap. His face started to get red; then a low-pressure area swept across it and he showed off his veneers; a set of even white teeth is to an investigative reporter what a good pair of orthopedic shoes is to a detective. "Go to hell, you gimpy son of a bitch. I wrote for the *News*, and I never got farther back than Section Three."

We shook hands. I'd done my Boy Scout duty, saving society from another newshound on the public dole; for the moment, anyway. That should have put a spring in my step. So why did I hobble out of there like a horse with a split hoof?

TWENTY-FIVE

It was one of those cockeyed days where the bright sun made you think you could shuck the jacket until you got outside, but not quite cold enough to run the heater, except to clear the fog that formed on the inside of the windshield when you breathed. After two minutes I switched it off and cranked the window down a couple of inches to equalize the pressure, or whatever the Weather Channel called it.

I had no place specific to go at that specific time. I was drifting with the current, which seemed to be flowing east-northeast along the big river. Anyway it was a route I'd traveled so many times the Cutlass practically made all the stops and turns for me, like a faithful old milk horse. That left time to wallow.

You were young for so long you took it for granted; you'd always be able to sprint, scale, take stairs three steps at a time, bend down and then stand straight without pulling yourself up hand over hand; middle-agers would go on calling you son. Then people began to retire: one by one to start, then in clumps, the way a sheepdog sheds in summer. Then before you knew it, you were attending more funerals than weddings. Turn around, and you were the last of something: the bison, the passenger pigeon, the Siberian tiger, the lamplighter, the private eye. They put your face on a commemorative stamp; doesn't matter that in America you don't rate that honor until you're dead. In the end all things are equal.

When I looked again, I was downtown, slowing to a stop in the blue zone in front of the Second Precinct. That made it perfect. The old gluepot always found its way back to the barn.

John Alderdyce stepped down to the sidewalk just as I drew the brake. He was dressed as he had been that morning, from a mannequin in the window of Ira's Big and Menacing. He saw me and crossed to the curb. I cranked my window the rest of the way down. "Not quitting time yet, Inspector. Making your own hours now?"

"That's what puts the special in Special Consultant. I was just headed down to the icebox to look at a stiff."

"He'll keep. I want to show you something." I reached back over the seat, scooped up the item, and stuck it out the window.

"It's a towel," he said. "I'll send you a bill for the expert opinion. What's the going rate with Chester Goss?"

"Funny you should say that." I waggled the terry bundle.

He took it and wrinkled his nose. "Who used it last, the Olympic team?"

"Just a guy playing catch with himself. It wouldn't be much good coming straight from the laundry."

"Oh. Cootie call. You going to tell me who, or do I ask them to match it to one in three hundred million just for practice?"

"Hop in. I'll drive you to the morgue."

"When you put it that way, who could resist?" He went around and climbed into the passenger's seat. A truckload of solid gristle and bone pressed the springs flat. I grabbed the shifting cane. A vise closed on my wrist.

"Not so fast. It's a short drive, and I smell a long story."

I pointed at the sign that read POLICE PARKING ONLY. "I could get ticketed."

"I'll fix it—if I like what I hear."

"That's one more expense I'll have to charge my client. This stiff you're on your way to see: Has it got three holes in its chest?"

A mountainous shoulder leaned against the back of his seat. The face that went with it had been blocked out with explosive charges; it was still awaiting the chisel to finish it off. "Ordinarily I'd ask if you made them, but I've got a preliminary report says different. Which one are you, Tonto or the Lone Ranger?"

"In this case Tonto. It's a good shoot, John. He upgraded from blunt instrument to a garage sale thirty-two overnight."

"Thirteen hours ago, to be precise. You spent only four of them not finding him in our files. Just in there." It was his turn to point, at the precinct house. "You work pretty fast yourself; when you're working for yourself and not the system of justice. Kopernick's got some filling in to do; especially if not all three of those slugs turn out to have come from his sidearm."

"They're all his." I indicated the towel in his lap with an elbow. "He called me down to the shack on Hastings to give me that. It belongs to Goss." I gave him the rest, beginning with the dead man on the floor and circling back to the towel. "He didn't tell me where he got it, or who from. I worked that out myself."

He only looked like a slab of igneous rock: The brain behind those ledges and hollows worked like a NASA control panel. "That's not just a leap," he said. "Evel Knievel wouldn't have made it halfway across." But the doubt in his tone was only general; there was no shock in it. As familiar as Barry Stackpole was with the worst in human nature, he was after all just a visitor. Alderdyce lived there. He was concerned only with repercussions.

"Kopernick got the idea from me," I said. "If I hadn't told him about Goss's genealogy kick, he never would have come to me with the towel."

"Why you? He hates P.I.s on principle, and you like a personal case of stomach cancer, and even if he didn't, only the department can order a DNA test."

"The department's already up to its elbows in one incident involving Kopernick and a place he wasn't assigned to while he was on duty. He's low on points when it comes to official cooperation, but if his hunch pays off, it could put him on the square, and with interest. He wouldn't ask, even if I was best man at his wedding, and he sure wouldn't admit it; but he wants me to grease this through. So do I." I gripped the wheel; that at least I could control. "I appreciate your help, but he's the only cop who's been willing to put his job on the block by letting this bee out of the jar."

"It was already on the block. He's snatching at straws." He crumpled the towel with one hand. "Without being able to explain how we got it and on what information, it isn't evidence; it's just a smelly rag. Even if it made it through channels, it's illegal search and seizure. 'Oops, my bad' might work for you, not for the department. Goss has the legal clout to sue the city for millions for defaming his sterling character. The city attorneys can't get them back from me, so they'll settle for my hide."

"Tell that to Goss. Who'd he call first? Not his lawyers. He thought that smelly rag was worth killing a cop to get it back." I told him about Kenneth Whitelaw.

"Was I going to get that at all?" he said when I finished. "Were you just holding it in reserve in case I needed the shove?"

"It's brand-new. I'm coming to you with it first. The only excuse Kopernick would've had for visiting Goss in his house so he could put that thing in your hands was to tell him he was turning down his job offer. I don't know if Goss missed the towel, but when he found out his bribe didn't work, he set his dog loose; his cutthroat dog. Same one he sent to toss my office to find out what I'd gathered."

I lifted my hands off the wheel. "Okay, it's not exactly ironclad. But how many coincidences have to pile up in order to see the fire for the smoke?"

"It's not even strong enough to *call* coincidence. Goss has exposed hundreds of crooks. How many of them have already migrated to Detroit once they were cut loose? Our fair town is a clearinghouse for every perp in the continental United States."

"And this one just happened to target me and Kopernick just when the April Goss case hotted up again." I squinted against that two-faced sun. "Do this," I said. "Find out who pulled what strings to spring Whitelaw before he served his full sentence. An endorsement from the celebrity who put him in the cage in the first place has to draw some water with a parole board."

"You and Kopernick. Jesus Christ. I'd sooner expect Iran and Israel to team up in a sack race."

"What can I say? He's kind of warm and fuzzy once you draw his fangs."

He sat back, gripping the towel with both hands. If we were moving and his window was open, I'm not sure he wouldn't have been tempted to chuck it out. His expression was bleak, not stricken. As I said, he'd seen the worst. "I can try sending it out as a John Doe. That's done sometimes in classified cases—I mean the red-hots—but it pisses off the smocks. Damn it, Walker! Ink's not dry on my reappointment, and you want to send me back to the shuffleboard court."

I made a sour face at the rearview. "Don't say 'retirement,' John. Anything but that."

"Bite me. You're all out of favors." He opened his door and got out.

"You don't want a ride?"

"Whitelaw can wait; that's what cadavers do best. I need to put this here key piece of evidence into official custody before it stinks up my best suit."

That was a curtain cue, and it was a dandy; but he didn't take it. Instead he tucked the towel under one arm and laid a hand on the dash. "Amos."

It got my attention. I could count on the fingers of one thumb the times he'd called me by my first name.

"If you're right—and you just might be, because a hunch is just a word for miles on the odometer—Goss isn't the kind to roll over after taking just one on the chin. What's the score now on his show, four figures?"

"About that. I'm two years behind."

"That's one deep bench of pinch-hitters for Whitelaw."

I grinned. "Worried about me?"

He shot straight up. "Have it your way. You always do. There are plenty enough slabs to go around." The door banged shut.

I sat there for a while, gripping the wheel with both hands like the ledge outside a penthouse window. Leave it to a cop to have more than one exit line.

TWENTY-SIX

The office looked pouty; I hadn't been in since the excitement, and with almost every independent contractor working at home these days, it wasn't sure I'd be in again ever. The magazines curling up their toes in the waiting room, the homely green file cabinets in the cloister, the schoolmarm's desk—even the tin Detroit Tigers wastebasket I punted when time grew heavy—greeted me without hope, like puppies in the pound. Probably it was just the stagnant air. I hoisted up the window to stick my face into the cold, breathe in diesel exhaust, and listen to the loose tappets playing drum solos two stories under my feet.

I sat down, propped my heels on a drawleaf, and shuffled through the mail I'd found under the slot. Someone wanted to sell me a walk-in bathtub, GM wanted to recall a Chevy I hadn't owned in twenty years (a faulty locknut that could dump the steering wheel in my lap at fifty miles per hour), a college student with faulty penmanship in Zimbabwe needed a thousand dollars to come to the United States and collect a half-million-dollar inheritance, I had an appointment coming up at the dentist's for a cleaning and checkup. Entering the last in my desk calendar, I poured myself a dram from the bottle I kept in the safe with the other hand: multi-tasking.

It was getting easier to swallow, but I was still wearing my tie at half-mast to accommodate the swollen muscle on the side of my neck. I wondered if I was getting slower to heal; but then I remembered all that was just last night. It was my biological clock that was on the blink, not my powers of recuperation. Which was more serious in a line of work that required both a sense of timing and a reasonable amount of indestructibility? I consulted the bottle again, and the anesthetic started to kick in.

That was my schedule for the afternoon.

It's not like it is in thrillers, an unbroken string of twists, turns, and traffic circles to keep the audience from running out for popcorn; should be, but it's not. An investigation is a long trudge through loose sand, and when you finish churning your way to the top of one dune, all you get is a view of the next. Then you run out of dunes.

I took my feet down from the desk and booted the wastebasket across the room. I was reduced to straining metaphors until they squeaked.

My glass was empty. It had a hole in it; the hole being on top. I tickled the bottle—foreplay—then screwed the cap back on, shut it in the safe, spun the dial, and shot to my feet. I let myself out, locking the door, then had to unlock it again to go back in and close the window. Sitting around doing nothing is a lot more entertaining when it's done at home.

I don't know why I bothered with the lock. I was the only one who needed a key to get in.

But I was locking up again when the telephone rang. I almost didn't go back for it; it was probably the receptionist at the dentist's office reminding me teeth didn't clean themselves.

I lost that battle too. It was still ringing when I got back inside and made a long arm across the desk.

"Mr. Walker? Oh, thank God!"

It was Chrys Corbeil. I stopped leaning and asked her what was wrong.

"Someone called from prison. Dan's in the infirmary. They said he attacked a guard."

We were practically neighbors. She rented the second floor of a row house in Hamtramck, one of the developments the city had thrown up under U.S. Grant to entice hardworking Poles and Ukrainians to come work for the railroads. When she saw me behind the wheel she left the wooden porch and climbed into the passenger's seat.

The bank had been closed for an hour. She was dressed for home, in a sweatshirt, chamois slacks respectably wrinkled, and scuffed loafers. Her hair was gathered behind her neck with a bandanna, pale yellow to match the hair. No purse. I don't know why women bother carrying them based on how many of them go without.

"They're expecting us; me, that is. I told them when they called I was on my way."

"Who called?" I found a hole in the homebound traffic and plugged it.

"Some woman, a secretary or something. I'm the only one on Dan's emergency contact list. Mr. Walker, why would he do it?"

"Tell me what and I'll try to work out why."

"She said he rushed the guard in the exercise yard. They carry those folding things now—"

"Batons."

"Yes. The guard swung it at his head. He's unconscious, under observation for signs of concussion. Mr. Walker, Dan's not violent, no matter what the jury thought. I've spoken to his counselors. They'll tell you his behavior has been good since the beginning. He must have been provoked."

"It happens. Some of them manage to get on the bad side even of a good guard, and there are bad guards who live for the chance to play with their toys. I'm not saying it's either of those things. Dan's been on a roller coaster this week. We're responsible for that, or at least I am. I took a convict without hope and turned him square around. Hope's a tricky thing. While he didn't have it, he at least knew where he stood. Now he's right back in that courtroom, waiting for the foreman to stand up and speak."

She looked at me. Those wide-set eyes were disconcerting. Inarguable innocence always is. It's like a crystal pitcher balanced on the edge of a table, ready to fall off at the slightest vibration. "Are you saying we're to blame?"

"Me more than you. Hell, just me. I should've seen it, but things on the outside don't look the same as they do when you're behind bars. Did they say he could see visitors?" I knew the answer to that; penal regulations are the same everywhere. A change of subject was necessary.

"No. I didn't think to ask. But there must be someone who can tell us what happened and whether—" A lip got bitten.

"Let's not borrow trouble. Turnkeys are trained in the use of force, how much to do the job and no more." I'd almost said "deadly force." I was sleep deprived, with no cure in sight.

The same woman in uniform who'd checked me out on my first visit recognized us both. That was impressive, at least where I was concerned. She'd seen me only twice, and Chrys was a regular. She looked less institutional this time. As often as it happened, an incident involving an inmate and a fellow guard shook up the faithful as regards the infallibility of the organization. "Mr. Otto wants to see you. He's our community director."

We followed a guard I hadn't seen before down a corridor that might have been the same one I'd been in before, but I couldn't swear to it. One taupe-colored passage looked pretty much like all the rest.

It wasn't the same one. This one led to a steel door enameled to look like wood that stood open several inches. He opened it wide enough for us to step through, my client first, and receded back into the system.

A mild-looking soul of fifty or so, with a graying moustache parted in the middle and swept to the sides, rose from behind a gray metal desk with a composition top. He arranged his hair the same way, but nature had taken hold of that and parted it like the Red Sea, plowing a pink path all the way to a bald crown. A trivet on the desk read VICTOR OTTO. He looked like a Victor the way I look like Miley Cyrus.

He buttoned his corduroy coat over a roll of dough and offered us each a hand. Chrys, anticipating tears, was gripping a lace-edged handkerchief, which she used to mop her palm when he gave it back. I wiped mine on my hip. If Otto saw it, he suppressed any reaction; that's what community directors do. He indicated a pair of metal folding chairs facing the desk. They were gray, which was the prevailing theme: file cabinets, carpet, walls, monochrome shots of Old Ypsilanti in pewter frames. It was life in a furnace duct.

When we were all uncomfortably seated, he said, "First things first. Mr. Corbeil is stable. He's regained consciousness, and the nurse on duty says his vitals are all sound. We're only keeping him in the infirmary overnight for observation."

Chrys said it first. "Nurse? Where's the doctor?"

"Home for the day. We called him there, but based on the report he's confident the staff can handle it without his presence. It's a capable staff," he said. "Very capable."

I asked him what happened.

He shifted in his seat, ran a finger along the edge of his desk and inspected it for dust. When he looked up, his eyes didn't shift so much as wander around, alighting on some object at rest or blank stretch of wall, which seemed to be where he found his words. "A mistake. Our man in the exercise yard reacted from training. His back was turned, and Mr. Corbeil, er, bumped into him. He responded in his own defense."

I said, "Bumped into him how?"

"Another inmate jostled Mr. Corbeil. He lost his balance and fell against the guard. Two witnesses came forward to tell us that later. I'm sorry that information wasn't available when we called you, Miss Corbeil."

So far he hadn't looked at me since we shook hands.

"Jostled how?" I said.

"We're still investigating that. Our witnesses say he tripped and ran into him from behind, shoulder-first. Clearly an accident, but as I said—"

"What's this klutz's name?"

"I can't tell you that, pending the results of our inquiry. We have a board—"

Chrys broke in. "Can I see my brother?"

"Of course, of course. Not today, though. He's conscious, but he's in no condition to receive visitors. Tomorrow, perhaps—"

She pounced; I squeezed her knee and she slid back two inches on her chair.

"Mr. Otto." I smiled. "I bet your friends call you Vic."

He nodded. He'd been about to pounce himself. I'd figured him to be longer on defense than offense, but there's only so much you can draw from a nervous manner and a soggy grip.

"Vic." I took out my ID folder and laid it open on the desk with the honorary sheriff's star showing, and I wasn't smiling now.

"I've been retained by Corbeil's attorney to review his case; according to the U.S. Constitution and the Michigan State Penal Code, that means I'm to have access to the client any time I ask. His sister has the same rights in case of emergency as next of kin. Corbeil's trial made a good-size splash in the media twenty years ago. You know how much those folks love to uncover old material

and serve it up fresh. Also they haven't had a violent incident behind bars to report all year."

He touched his moustache to make sure it hadn't slipped. Well,
I hadn't expected him to turn green and start speaking in tongues;
he was too experienced a bureaucrat. He flipped a toggle and gave
the necessary instructions to the voice on the other end of the intercom. Two minutes later yet another guard appeared to conduct
us to the infirmary.

TWENTY-SEVEN

A pair of plain wood doors with rubber bumpers designed for shoving gurneys through opened into a facility indistinguishable from any other hospital, if you discounted uniformed security stationed at both ends of the wide, linoleum-paved corridor, thumbs hooked inside leather tool belts hung with standard police paraphernalia, minus the ballistics; but then if things kept going the way they had been, that particular addition would be just as visible everywhere soon.

Portable units formed alcoves on both sides of the hallway; glorified pipe racks on casters with flimsy curtains hanging from them, some closed, with dim figures lying in hospital beds in some of the open ones. There was the usual ambient noise of electronic monitors beeping when reporting blood pressure, rubber-wheeled carts squeaking on the waxed tiles in parallel corridors, filters humming as they cleaned the air of dust and harmful agents. Ceiling LEDs shed even light throughout.

A nurse—identifiable by her flowered smock and thirty pounds of unhealthy extra weight—sat at a small metal desk just inside the doors, conversing in a monotone with someone on the other end of a phone. She glanced up at us, plainly irritated by the intrusion, but when the guard whispered, "Corbeil," her expression shifted into neutral. I showed her the pass Victor Otto had given us, a white sheet of memo paper bearing the date, time, and his signature, a scribble that wandered all over the place, like his eyes. With her hand cupped over the mouthpiece, she said, "Three."

Pale blue cardboard squares were clipped to the curtains belonging to the alcoves, with numbers on them in black marker. The guard led us to number three, which was open, said, "Visitors," and left us.

He was sitting up in bed, hooked to a monitor by a clothespin on his index finger, with a square patch of gauze taped to a patch that had been shaved just forward of his right temple, wearing a thin cotton gown under a pale blue blanket drawn up to his sternum. He was pale, but all things considered his look was an improvement over the first time we'd met. It wasn't the greasy pallor he'd worn then, but more in keeping with a man who'd sustained a recent injury, and it seemed he'd filled out some since we'd conferred for the second time, in his cell. His eyes were bright as ever above the dark circles. The corners of his lips actually turned up when he recognized his sister.

"Dan." She touched the hand wired up to the machine, which chose that moment to beep and display his blood pressure, 168 over 62. It was more comforting not to assign that to coincidence, so I kept my mouth shut when her eyes flicked that way, glowing perceptibly.

"Hey." His voice was hoarse; but this time it didn't seem as if he'd just taken it out of months of mothballs. His eyes drifted my way, changed slightly.

I said, "How's the food?"

He looked back at Chrys. "What's he doing here?"

She and I traded glances. It was as if the blow to the head had erased our last talk.

"He drove me," she said. "How are you?"

"They come and go."

"Who comes and goes, Dan?"

He smiled again. "The Blue Meanies."

Another exchange with Chrys, smiling now too. It was that neo-hippie upbringing they shared. Their past ran from Liverpool to Yoko Ono: Not one day before or after.

He went on. "They come the first day and stay for a while. Then they sort of fade off. Then they come on and off, for twenty years and counting."

The subject was prison life, not the knock on the noggin.

A throat cleared; not his. We looked at a compact figure in a baggy white coat over prison denims: an orderly and a trusty. He might have been thirty-five or fifty, dark brown hair mowed close to the scalp, his nose all over his face, and tapes of scar-tissue around his eyes. It was a face that had seen even more action than mine.

"Everything okay here?" He had a high, piping tenor, as if someone had removed the voice box of a light middleweight and replaced it with one from the lead singer of a doo-wop band.

I said, "Tell Nurse Ratched we're fine."

There was a chair in the room, a thing of plastic and aluminum that wouldn't make much of a weapon. He slid it out into the hall and sat, resting his broken-knuckled hands on his knees. "He's sorry. The guard is. I believe him. He's one of the better ones. He acted from reflex."

I looked at Chrys, nodded. She responded and leaned lower over her brother, talking not much above a whisper. I stepped out of the alcove and slid the curtain around the track, between brother and sister and P.I. and convict. It wouldn't cut off sound, but it created a psychological separation.

I stood close enough to the orderly to talk quietly, but far enough away so he didn't have to crane his neck to look up at me. Put my hands in my pockets. "What happened in the yard?"

"What did they tell you?

"Another inmate tripped, fell against him, and pushed him against a guard."

"That's what they said."

His face was blank behind its mask of healed-over flesh. I usually keep a ten-spot in a pocket: In case of emergency, break glass. I brought it out folded in my palm and shook his hand. He laid it back on his knee with nothing showing.

"Ever been in an exercise yard?"

I didn't answer. When a high-pitched voice whispers, it's like air escaping from a tea-kettle. I had to lean forward to make out the words.

"There's nothing to trip on," he said. "If there was, some con would pick it up and clobber somebody with it. I go out there sometimes after lockdown, for fresh air when I pull an all-nighter here. The ground's smooth as a skating rink, only a hell of a lot less slippery. Not slippery at all."

Fresh air. I recognized his cologne: *Tank* was the name. It's targeted at college students to kill the odor of beer and entry-level employees to avoid triggering a urine test for pot. He didn't look the least bit academic.

"What's the clumsy one's name?" I said.

He shook his head. I was fresh out of quick-draw tens. I reached for my wallet, but he shook his head.

"I stole a car," he said; "I was high, not stupid. There's guys in here, they was in Texas or Oklahoma, place like that, they'd be waiting for the needle. You can only be stuck once, and you can only be sent up for one lifetime."

"What about the guard?"

"He regrets it. I said that. He's okay, or as okay as they ever get. Some of 'em, that happened, your friend wouldn't be in here with a bump on his skull. He'd be in the basement. You know the basement?"

"Sure. You don't store stiffs where a visiting civilian might run into them. So why did our friend who's lucky he wasn't in Texas or Oklahoma pick a tame turnkey instead of a yard bull with an attitude?"

"Your guess is as good as mine. All I know is that's what they did this time."

I nodded. "This time."

He rolled his head on his neck. It sounded like someone stepping on a bag of potato chips. "Next time, who knows? He could stumble into one that just had a fight with his wife."

"A Blue Meanie."

His face didn't get any less blank. I pegged him for an Elvis man.

He got up from the chair, put the hand that had been hiding the bill into a pocket; stuck the other hand in his other pocket; a casual attitude, for the benefit of the guard at either end of the corridor. "There's no privacy in a ward like this," he said. "Your friend needs a private room. I wouldn't wait."

I watched him walking away, on the balls of his feet like a man with plenty of experience in the ring. Then I ducked my head around the curtain. Chrys was still holding her brother's hand, her face close to his. If they were conversing at all, it was too low to hear from more than three feet away. The position she was in, down on one knee, looked uncomfortable, but she was half my age, and her gender bends more easily in some places than mine. Anyway I swung the chair inside and set it down as quietly as possible; she could do with it what she liked. Then I backed off and let the curtain drop. They'd be busy for a while.

Victor Otto was still at his desk, making small crabbed notations in the margins of a presentation or something; that seemed to be part of the job description of a community director. When he looked up and saw me, he wore the expression of a man who'd just been told his cancer was no longer in remission.

I told him I wanted two more things. This time his show of resistance closed before the end of the first act.

TWENTY-EIGHT

I t wasn't an accident, was it?"

We were on our way back to Detroit. It was the first she'd spoken since we left Huron Valley. She'd been looking at the scenery sliding past, not seeing it. Now she was looking straight ahead through the windshield, and not seeing anything there either.

I'd been expecting the question. She was just finishing her visit when the nurse appeared with the orderly I'd spoken to, to unhook Dan Corbeil from the monitor, transfer him to a gurney, and wheel him down the hall and through another set of doors—steel this time, with STAFF ADMITTANCE ONLY stenciled on them. Beyond them was another ward, restricted to a handful of inmates, with a guard assigned to each around the clock; this much I'd gotten from Otto, once he'd agreed to authorize the transfer.

"No," I said to Chrys. "He'll be safe in that area. When he's back on his feet, they'll put him in isolation." I told her the story behind the ten dollars I was adding to expenses.

"You mean solitary? The hole?"

I had to grin. "You should switch to the Hallmark Channel. 'The hole' went out with Free Dish Night. That kind of punishment never did work anyway. He'll have all the amenities of his regular cell and the yard to himself and his own private turnkey for company."

"But why would anyone want to hurt Dan? Does it have to do with you looking into his case?"

"It has everything to do with it. Someone's sending a message: Lay off, or the next one's for keeps."

She opened her mouth, but I interrupted her before anything came out.

"Before you have second thoughts, think. It means Dan's innocent. Only the guilty party would go to such lengths to stop the investigation."

"That's nothing new. I know he's innocent. I've known it all along. That's why I hired you."

"You hired me to reopen the case. You were convinced he'd been framed; that's not the same thing as knowing. I said at the time I'd keep working it till I was satisfied one way or the other. Now I am. Too many people are interested in something that was supposed to have been settled four presidential administrations ago."

"So what happens now?"

"I wound up some little mechanical men and sent them out in several directions before I got your call. Now I'm going to start gathering them up to see what they brought back."

The first one answered to the name Barry. After I dropped Chrys off at her place I speed-dialed him. "Not retired yet?" I said.

"Screw you. Just when I think I'm out, you drag me back in. Guess who added his two cents to Kenneth Whitelaw's parole hearing?"

"Name rhyme with Chester Goss?"

"He submitted a stack of letters written in pencil on yellow notepaper, along with the envelopes they came in, stamped and canceled. All in the same hand, with the same signature. Whitelaw can't spell for shit, but he spent a fair amount of his time in the

Atlanta pen writing thank-you notes to Goss in care of the show, and making his case."

"'Bless me, for I have sinned'?"

"Bingo. Struck just the right balance between maudlin and calculating. More on the first side as the correspondence went on, less on the second. A man coming to believe his own publicity. I tell you, if I was chief financial officer of a chain of supermarkets putting in some of my spare time serving the community on a parole board, I'd've asked for a Kleenex."

"What about his record inside?"

"Clean enough. Some contraband, non-lethal, non-drug-related; be suspicious if there weren't something like that in his jacket. Just because he's crude don't mean he ain't shrewd. Like a schizo that knows how to appear sane when it counts."

"Thin, even to a supermarket suit. What clinched it?"

"Gainful employment. Goss brought an affidavit signed by him, promising to hire Whitelaw as a stringer as soon as he was sprung."

"What's a stringer?"

"Journalese, sorry. A regional source of leads that might prove interesting to a wide audience."

"You mean a snitch."

"A snitch with a press pass. You know, like an associate with an escort service instead of a ten-dollar whore. Three hundred a week to start, and a C-note every time he reported something the show could use. Travel expenses, too, if it's meaty enough to bring him north to discuss details."

"Details such as tossing my office to see what I'd dug up and dry-gulching Kopernick after he told Goss thanks but no thanks on the job offer."

"That's the theory. I can download all this from my source in Dixie and bring it over or snail-mail it to you for your records."

"Not necessary. It wouldn't prove anything except to you and me. But since you've got that much energy—"

"Palm trees can wait, that it?" But he didn't sound peeved; once a bloodhound's got the scent, you can't stop him with a two-by-four.

"Hang on." I turned into my driveway. My house was only a few blocks from Chrys's. "This one's public record. That means you can put your spies to rest. I don't want to bother Alderdyce with it; he's busy balancing his career on his thumb as it is, as a favor to me."

"Horseshit. He hands out favors like the Grinch hands out candy canes."

I thought about that. "Grinch; not bad. Not good, either. It's all in the interest of justice, Barry. It could turn out I'm the generous one."

"Spill it."

I told him what I wanted. There was no pause when I finished, to take notes. If I had his memory I'd work onstage. "Where'd you get this?"

"From a little gray man in a little gray office."

"When do you need it? Don't say yesterday. I'd say buy me a time machine."

"Today, then."

"Go to hell."

Men with his talent were sensitive about being taken for granted. I said, "Call me at home; landline. This one has me burning through minutes like napalm."

He didn't call. I was sitting in the easy chair wondering if the ice in my glass would stand another soaking when the doorbell rang. It kept on ringing until I opened the door because Barry was leaning against the button. He knew I hated that.

"I hope you got more ice." He indicated the glass in my hand, using the manila file folder he'd brought in for a pointer. "You know what kind. I prefer my liquor unscorched."

I found a tombstone-shaped bottle in the kitchen cupboard behind a jar of mayonnaise. It was Gentleman Jack. I couldn't remember who gave it to me. Bourbon's best for pouring on waffles.

I gave him the easy chair. It needed as many backsides as possible to rearrange the broad hollow Stan Kopernick had left in the cushion. He accepted a glass and I sat on the love seat facing him, jingling the fresh cubes in my Scotch. I pointed at the folder in his lap. "You could've given me that over the phone. I didn't need it in writing."

"I sweep *my* phone. Any kid could tap that old rotary of yours with a pipe cleaner and a pair of alligator clamps. You said yourself Goss is wired to the Department. Why stop there?"

"I keep forgetting to ask Alderdyce about that. This is no ordinary link. He gets his information too fast." I kept staring at the folder. I hadn't touched my drink yet.

He touched his, set it down on the end table by the chair, and leaned forward to pass me the file.

I opened it, looked at the front-and-profile photo printed out on top. This boy was no Kenneth Whitelaw. He wore dreadlocks and a scowl that would curdle milk. The swastika carved in each meaty cheek was superfluous. "Half Rastafari, half White Power. How'd he last this long?"

"Fact he has says as much about him as his sheet. Spoiler alert: It ends with him doing ninety-nine years and a day for triple murder. If they'd made all the others stick, he'd be serving real time."

"Pro?"

"All-star. Started with the Colombian cartel, Miami end. He scared them so much they imported a death squad from Bogota to wipe him out; he killed three of 'em before he decided to come north for his health. Not so healthy for the heavyweights he ran afoul of in L.A., East St. Louis, Chicago, and some gangbangers here at home.

"Young Boys Incorporated?"

"There never was a Young Boys Incorporated. That was old Mayor Young's invention, like his Form 1040. They're what this prize package took the fall for: He used a welding torch on a big-time dealer, but not before he broke into his crib and cut the heads off the dealer's girlfriend and her little boy. He let the dealer see his work before he fired up the acetylene."

"Guess he wasn't so clumsy then." I skimmed an arrest report. "Jared Kady. That's not the name I gave you."

"You're looking at an old beef. Last page."

I shuffled to the back. "Abrahim Ibn Said."

"Had it changed legally when he converted. Only legal thing he ever did, I'm guessing. Even the Taliban refused to claim credit for him. Terrorist without portfolio."

"Been bingeing *Cutthroat Dogs*?"

"Hard to stop. Goss devoted two episodes to him solo. Another guess? Drugs in stir. A lot of smart prison reformers have wasted a lot of time trying to stop the flow from outside. There's even an unwritten rate sheet: Broken leg, half a kilo of crack; morgue job, two rocks of H. Goss's tipsters have put enough mules inside for him to arrange regular delivery, just like Amazon."

"How much of that can we prove?"

"Zilch."

I riffled the pages. They made a nasty sound, like a buzzing rattlesnake. "No wonder my orderly wouldn't finger him by name; but he was short on imagination. Said he won't try the same thing a second time. He doesn't need a mean guard with a hair trigger to take out Corbeil. He'll handle it himself."

"Think he will?"

"The orderly was right about one thing. This state hasn't had the death penalty for two hundred years. They can't send you up for life twice."

TWENTY-NINE

I made him a present of the bottle of bourbon on his way out. "Put it in the trunk, Barry. An open-intoxicants bust will retire you for sure."

After he left, I squirmed around in the armchair, rolling my glass between my palms and massaging my cortex with invisible fingers. In the middle of this a horn blasted five times in the street out front. When I got my heart jacked down from my windpipe, I went to the door, picking up my .38 on the way.

A gray Ford Taurus sat alongside the curb on the wrong side of the street. Only a cop has that attitude toward the law, and only John Alderdyce would call attention to it by honking. I stuck the revolver under my belt in the small of my back and approached the open window on the driver's side. His eyes glowed in the twilight like a cat's.

He said, "One order of DNA, hot from the oven. This the right address?"

"What's the name on the order?"

"I'll spell it. G—"

I trotted around and let myself into the seat beside him.

He looked at me, eyes bright under the rocky mantel of his brow. "The towel tested positive against his sample on file with the feds, and it's all over the physical evidence in storage from the April Goss investigation."

I sat back against the seat. "He claimed he'd never been in the apartment."

"Twice. The first time, all there was to go on was fingerprints, and they'd been wiped off both doorknobs and impossible to re-cover from the razor blade she was supposed to have used to slash her wrists. That was clever, smearing the prints on the murder weapon so it would look like the killer tried to make it look like a case of suicide, but obliterating them entirely from the doorknobs to make the first assumption fall through. *This* time there was no excuse except the cocky son of a bitch didn't think we'd check back; or that we couldn't. He spent a whole episode last year reviewing the department's sloppy handling of rape-test kits and other evidence in mothballs."

"Lot of trouble to go through just because he and his daughter didn't get along."

"It might have been worse than that—the worst, if you get my meaning."

I nodded. "I thought of that, too."

"Then again, they might have fought, he shoved her, and she bumped her head on something. The coroner found a bruise on the occipital lobe—not enough to cause death, but maybe it looked like it in his panic. The rest was cover-up."

"In which case all you've got on him is Man Three and tamper-ing with evidence. Without proof he rigged the system so the jury didn't know April wasn't pregnant—which would have weakened Corbeil's motive—you can't even connect him to a frame. Corbeil's prints were all over the rest of the apartment. As of course they would be, since he and April were in a relationship."

"It's a start."

"You'll be lucky to make even that stick. He's loaded, but he doesn't have to be to beat this case. He's got a premium network in love with his ratings. They'll buy him the best legal talent in the hemisphere. If they find out how Kopernick came by that towel, your probable cause to pull his DNA file goes out the window, and that whole line of evidence will be inadmissible. He'll know you don't have the cards to sweat the truth out of him."

Alderdyce's hands were on the steering wheel. He opened them, flexed the fingers, and took up the grip again. "It's a thin thread, no argument."

"Not just in the view of a judge," I said. "It doesn't wash any way I look at it. I don't like him, hate how he manipulates due process like it's his own set of Hot Wheels, but I don't see him as a wild animal who'd kill his kid in cold blood, or who wouldn't come clean if it was accidental."

We might be able to weave it into a string. You remember Officer Cochran?"

I didn't at first. "Glee club kid that printed me when I was brought in on the shooting in the bank; the one kept feeding me mug books after my run-in with Whitelaw in my office. Belongs in Pop's Chock'lit Shoppe, not the CID."

"Not the CID, anyway." He turned his head my way; the Cheshire Cat carved out of granite.

That time I was even slower on the uptake. I nodded, and went on nodding until I realized I hadn't stopped. "I was just saying to someone there's a larger-than-usual leak in the department. How'd you connect Cochran to Goss?"

"Goss's place is over the county line; those calls show up on record. In the last two weeks, twenty-seven calls were placed to his number, from a phone usually reserved for arrestees to call their lawyers or whatnot. He thought it wouldn't be monitored like the others. He was wrong; and he was seen using it more than once. A caller who doesn't want to be overheard tends to stand with his back to the rest of the room. We've got some personnel that are cop enough to know that."

"Not conclusive."

"Cochran didn't know that. Or felt too guilty to take it into account. He cracked when the guy from Internal Standards asked him his name. We're putting him on unpaid suspension. It's up to the brass whether to press charges."

"What'd Goss promise him, stringer?"

"What's a stringer?"

"Ask Barry. I didn't understand it myself."

"Expert consultant," he said.

I grinned. "He draws that like a gun. He might as well have offered him head of security, like me, only I'm realistic enough not to fall for it. How'd a simp like that make it through the training course?"

"Maybe his mother bribed the instructor, like they do in Hollywood." A pair of massive shoulders lifted, fell. It's a wonder the ground didn't shake. "It's a rotten world."

"Not entirely. For every one of those, there's a Chrys Corbeil."

"I'd argue the math. It's happening on some police force somewhere every day of the week. About as sensational as cheating on your taxes. *Cutthroat Dogs* wouldn't give it a tumble."

It hit me then. I was CID material myself, if you swung the shovel hard enough and knew where to aim.

THIRTY

"That's almost as hard to swallow as the other," he said after a moment.

"Almost."

"It's upside-down. Who'd buy it?"

"Us, for two. It makes Goss less of a monster. Ogre, maybe. Or a dog. Just not the cutthroat kind."

I watched him boring holes through the windshield with his eyes. The greenish dashboard lights reflected off his features, like neon off cast iron. The motor was still running. It was as if it had forgotten it was still running, not that he'd neglected to turn it off. It was his personal car, not an unmarked city unit, with rear, front, and side-mounted cameras. You'd have to be invisible to sneak up on us and eavesdrop, yet we were talking almost in whispers; the subject was that volatile.

Someone had to break the silence. That was me. "It's far-fetched. Yesterday I'd've passed it by like the front page of the *National Enquirer*. Compared to what we've been kicking around, I'd take it even if I couldn't prove it."

He said, "I don't like hypotheticals. They're worse than conspiracy theories. If we can't prove it, why waste time?"

"Maybe we can get him to furnish the proof. Did you tell young Cochran not to leave town?"

"No, and I didn't tell him to freeze either. Try to stay in this century. Dumb fuck that he is, he knows better than to skip under just the threat of indictment. That would seal the deal."

I told him what I had in mind. He heard me out; opened and closed his fists on the wheel again.

I got tired of waiting for him to answer. My patience was no match for his. "Think he'll go for it?"

"Depends on whether I can scare him enough. It's shaky as hell. The prosecutor would need plenty of convincing to push a case against an officer that's too weak to stick. There might not even be a crime. The April Goss investigation wasn't reopened, officially, so it isn't a matter of sharing confidential information with a civilian; which in itself isn't technically illegal."

"He confessed to bribery."

"He wasn't under oath. Any lawyer would advise him to recant. Even if he didn't, Goss would deny it, and then it's a rookie's word against a solid citizen's, and a public figure to boot."

"Cochran's a dope. If you lean hard enough, he won't have time to think it through. He doesn't have the equipment."

He looked at me sideways. "I thought you said it wasn't such a rotten world."

"Stupid's not rotten. It's common as dandelions, and we live with those. You just have to be scary enough: Freddy Krueger meets the Headless Horseman. You can do it, John," I said when he turned my way. "You're doing it now."

"Stop buttering me up. I can't pull this off solo. I'll need a Jekyll to my Hyde."

"Use Kopernick. He should be in on the kill. He's earned it."

"Uh-uh. That's bad cop, worse cop." He threw the car into gear. "Put on your game face. You're my first-round draft pick."

At night, Geronimo Circle was an oasis of gentle, slightly pinkish light, provided by carriage-type lamps mounted on poles. It was still early, and most of the houses were lit up, set each in its own private space, a marvel of geometrical logistics that created the illusion of country homes miles apart. The Gosses' low stone house was no exception, but only one window was illuminated. That seemed strange for a place where two people lived. There's usually some traffic between living room and kitchen, and only the obsessively frugal bothered to turn off the light in one room when leaving it for another. The host of a popular nationally televised reality show didn't pinch pennies, at least not in that area.

I parked against the curb a couple of houses down, cut the ignition and my lights, and sat for a while, smoking and listening to the motor making ticking noises as it cooled. I needed the quiet time. The session with Officer Cochran had wrung me out. Playing the nice guy, calling a suspect quietly by his first name, patiently lecturing his partner to keep cool, takes energy; especially when the suspect is as dumb as a doorstop and makes you want to yank off his clip-on tie and shove it down his throat. By comparison, Alderdyce, having gotten the poison out of his system grabbing the twerp by the hair and shouting into his ear, had emerged from the scene in a dream state, like someone stepping out of a hot tub. For him it was office routine, like sorting paperclips.

But the job was done. Provided it stayed that way.

My last drag took the cigarette down to the letters. I cracked the window and snapped out the butt. It made an orange arc in the darkness outside the nearest pool of salmon-colored light and blinked out on the dew-damp asphalt. I jerked the key out of the ignition, tipped up the door handle, and got out: the unchanging routine, so familiar I usually wouldn't remember doing it; tonight, every little step remained separate and worth concentrating on. It's always that way en route to the finish.

If it was the finish. It depended on too many things not to threaten to turn under on one little detail; like that one lonely window alight in the house cohabited by Chester and Vail Goss.

I climbed out of the car, stretched, popping every joint involved and a few that weren't, and strolled along the sidewalk toward the house. In neighborhoods like that, strolling is the gait to use after dark. Between the baleful single eye of the Neighborhood Watch and police patrols timed to the minute, a brisk pace or furtive behavior was liable to bring down the hammer of God. In any case I was in no hurry. If I took enough time, maybe a tornado or a nuclear attack would intervene and spare me the agony of a showdown. You could work it out in your head beforehand, plan your own moves and anticipate your opponent's, and all your opponent had to do was kick over the board. No battle plan ever survives the first engagement with the enemy.

It was a mild evening. For the first time since October I couldn't see my breath. I left my topcoat unbuttoned and let the tails spread before a breeze from the south. Crickets chirped, frogs sang on the margins of municipal retention ponds; whistling past the graveyard. But then maybe they didn't know how many more times they'd have to freeze before winter gave out.

The gong when I pressed the bell this time sounded sharper, like a coin striking the concrete floor of a huge empty warehouse. Goss must have been waiting for it. The door swung open before it died.

"'You jumped the shark,'" he said.

He was dressed for home, in a Lions jersey, the trousers from an old suit, and tasseled suede slippers. The light coming from an overhead fixture softened the pleats in his face.

I'd called ahead, using those same four words. Now I said, "Friendly warning. When Fonzie sailed over a shark on water skis, *Happy Days* was on its way out. Most of what I know about the entertainment industry I got from *TV Guide*. The trouble with having a popular series is you're always only one shark away from cancellation. Are you alone?"

"Vail's visiting her aunt in Toledo. An old friend of her mother's, actually, no relation." He turned from the door. His name was lettered on the back of the jersey.

For a television personality, he was an unaccomplished liar. He'd given me too much information about something that meant nothing to me; so of course now it did. Whether he'd gotten her out of the house so he could meet with me privately or she'd left on her own, it amounted to the same thing. Here and now was the border crossing, the point of fracture, the end of one thing and maybe the beginning of another.

I followed him from the green-and-white-tiled foyer through an unfamiliar doorway into a big living room with a high copper-coffered ceiling, deep armchairs, and a hearth faced in onyx or black marble, with a fire laid but not burning. Thick throw rugs made rectangular patterns on a floor built of broad planks.

A sleek silver box with twin speakers buzzed and crackled on a bookshelf. The volume was turned down so low the voice transmissions blended in with the static. He would have a police scanner. He would deduct it as a business expense.

"Drink?" He swung down a drop-leaf shelf belonging to an antique radio-phonograph cabinet, exposing a bank of bottles and assorted cocktail glasses.

"No thanks," I said. "Empty stomach."

"Cheese? Crackers? Vail's the cook, but she always leaves me with survival items."

"Pass." There's a point in every job where I like to have the blood flowing to my brain instead of my gut.

He poured something amber into a cut-crystal Old Fashioned, squirted in seltzer from a leaded glass bottle, and tipped a palm toward one of the armchairs. He sat facing me, crossing his legs and balancing his glass on his knee with a finger on the rim.

"I didn't figure you for a deep thinker. Not that you're dumb.

The reason I offered you that security job is you strike me as the type that acts from instinct, and fills in the rest after the crisis is past."

"That wasn't the reason."

He took a sip. Something crackled; not ice in the glass, because there wasn't any. The air was full of electricity; the on-and-off crackling from the scanner made it worse. I missed Vail Goss; more specifically, the wary calm she surrounded herself with, wary but stoic, a cloak against the elements. Chester wasn't using his TV voice—Rod Serling marinated in Lester Holt—but there was an edge to him tonight. Not the confrontational one that had ended our first meeting, but something submerged and waiting to breach. It sucked all the oxygen out of the room.

I was feeding it, of course. It had started with my phone call to let him know I was coming, and now that I saw how successful it was my game plan opened before me like a carpet runner unrolling down a steep flight of stairs.

I shoveled on more coal. "As much as you know about crime, you're an amateur at it in practice. If you hadn't told me you air an annual rehash of material from the past season, I'd still be picking through five years of episodes. That shortcut led me straight to Kenneth Whitelaw."

"I heard he was identified." He tilted his head toward the scanner. "If you say he showed up on the program, I'll have to take your word for it. They all run together after all this time, unless they have a reason to stand out."

"Like Abrahim Ibn Said. He earned the two full hours you spent on him. A guy like him would keep bin Laden awake nights."

His face smoothed out. In anyone else it would have been a sudden pallor. But his expression remained politely interested.

"I guess your man in the department didn't get around to telling you Dan Corbeil's attacker was identified."

"He was attacked?" He'd collected himself. He was an experienced interviewer, after all. No matter how unexpected the answer is to a question you asked, you must never show confusion. "Is he—?"

A phone rang. It couldn't have come at a better moment. I'd had a hell of a time not sneaking a look at my watch waiting for it.

THIRTY-ONE

The phone stood at attention on a base at Goss's elbow. As it rang, a robotic female voice announced that it was a Michigan call.

He waited for the answering machine to pick up. I'd expected that. In our state, "Michigan call" could mean a friendly canned sentiment from your local congressman or a bail request from your grandson being held in an Albanian prison. The line the suckers use at Second Precinct Admissions was separate from the official-business line.

"Mr. Goss?" said a youthful voice. "This is Coc—"

He snatched up the handset. "Not now." A beat. "Okay, what?"

I reached behind myself to scratch my back, loosening the Ruger in its holster while I was at it.

I had to admire his control. Aside from turning his glass around and around in his hand, he showed no reaction to what Officer Cochran was telling him. After a minute he said "Okay" again and replaced the handset. He uncrossed his legs, crossed them the other way. His face was illegible, but the new position reeked of smugness.

"Good news?" I said.

He drank. "Nothing I didn't expect. What you were saying. You think I had something to do with this Abrahim person?"

"Let's call him Jared Kady. Even radical Islam won't claim him.

He came through for you: Message received. If Corbeil's case stays open, next time he won't be so lucky. Same basic lesson I was supposed to learn from Whitelaw. Kopernick too, only that time he dropped the ball. Or was he supposed to finish the job after Kopernick turned down your offer?"

He set his glass on the pedestal table by the phone, put his foot back on the floor, and leaned forward, clasping his hands. His face remained immobile. "Do me a favor. Repeat what you just said before witnesses. My sponsors will love the free publicity when I take you to court."

"Then you'd force me to make my case. Slander's the only complaint where the rule of law doesn't apply to the defendant. The accused is challenged to prove his innocence, not the complainant to prove his guilt. I'd subpoena the tapes of the shows about Kady and Whitelaw and put Corbeil on the stand. It's circumstantial, yeah; but you know what Oscar Wilde said about the trout in the milk."

"It was Thoreau. You should check your sources before you enter a quote into evidence."

Triumph had seeped into his tone. It had nothing to do with catching me in an error. I smiled.

"Cochran lied," I said.

The mask cracked wide open. "What?"

"You'd have been proud of him when we braced him, Alderdyce and I. He held out a lot longer than we expected. I thought I'd be here at least an hour earlier. But the bluff worked in the end. He agreed to place that call so he could resign from the force instead of being dismissed for cause, and for a promise not to prosecute.

"You were bluffing, too," I said. "He wouldn't survive a week as an expert consultant on your show. When you fired him, all you had to do to shut him up was remind him you offered him a bribe and he took it."

He'd recovered some of his composure. "You're still bluffing. What is it you said he lied about? To me, you mean?"

"Corbeil. Cochran told you he just died of a cerebral hemorrhage brought on by that blow from a baton when Kady shoved him into the guard. We told him to say that. Corbeil's recovering, under constant surveillance for his protection. When he leaves the infirmary he'll be placed in isolation. We put a muzzle on your cutthroat dog Kady."

"What was the point of the call? Is that why you said you'd put him on the stand? Make me drop my guard, say or do something to incriminate myself because I thought he couldn't testify?"

"An experienced talking head like you? Come on. I just wanted to see how you'd take the news. I had to be sure I was right about you."

"I'm listening."

"Of course you are. You're a professional interviewer." I rearranged myself again, leaning forward like him to keep from pinning the revolver to the back of my chair. "Everyone was so caught up in the story that Corbeil murdered April and rigged the scene to look like suicide. What the hell, writers have been using that one for a hundred years. Cops love it when real-life killers try to imitate it. It's so obvious, with certain evidence conveniently removed so that it couldn't have been suicide, it greased the prosecution's case. Only it didn't happen that way. Exactly the opposite.

"I can't even say you blundered," I said. "Twenty years ago, who could've predicted forensic science would come into a windfall like DNA?"

"And just how did I betray myself, according to you?"

"That wooden-Indian act of yours can work two ways. Guy calls, reports something grim—only not so grim for you—you don't ask questions, tell him he's got a wrong number; you don't even show surprise. Which you would, if you had any notion I knew what the call was about. How could you? You didn't know

I'd helped coach him what to say, and was expecting the call when it came.

"Sometimes," I said, "subtle shouts."

He said nothing; sat back again and steepled his hands like a priest in the box.

I went on. "Alderdyce said my theory was upside-down. I had more than half a mind to agree with him. It was like saying wet sidewalks cause rain. But I couldn't let go of it, and that's what convinced me in the end. No matter how many times you push things away, the one that keeps coming back is the truth."

"And what truth is that?"

"It wasn't murder made to look like suicide. It was suicide made to look like murder."

He separated his hands, recrossed his legs, and picked up his drink. He was back in charge, the host of the program. "And why would I do that? Go to all that trouble just to spare April's memory? That's not even a motive. It's a joke."

"That's what I thought, so I threw it out and got another. Two, actually. Oldest in the book. *The* Book, in fact. Fear and greed.

"Fear first. How does a parent whose daughter kills herself come off? Either someone who didn't care enough about his own child to read the signs beforehand or a tyrant who drove her to it. The cops would look into that. Even if they didn't find anything to back it up, the specter of abuse—physical, emotional, sexual—would still be out there in the public eye. Even a minor celebrity like the host of a local cable-access TV show would feed that hunger. People love it when someone famous turns out to be a louse. The cops would drop the investigation for lack of evidence; but not before your sponsors dropped you.

"Or maybe it'd be worse," I went on; "no one would care. You'd be just another weak character whose kid wouldn't even go to him with her troubles. She'd been diagnosed as a depressive once, and even though she was declared cured, it's a condition that can come back, like malaria. It made more sense for her to slash her wrists than to depend on you to snap her out of it. And then you'd be somebody who used to be sort of famous, and now just some loser, only nobody cared. What could be worse for a spotlight hound like you?"

Here was another place where his poker face worked against him. I'd started out groping my way into it, still unconvinced even that late in the game; but as I moved on to the brutal details of April's death, he gave me nothing to show they pained him at all. And I knew then I'd scored a hit.

"No," I said, "suicide would be a disaster. But a watchdog for justice whose daughter was murdered by her boyfriend—that's gold in terms of ratings. A grieving father who throws all that attention into ramming through a conviction; a crusader with a personal grudge against crime. Guy like that deserves a bigger audience. Motive number two: greed.

"April's neighbor wasn't the first to discover her body," I continued. "You were. Maybe you went there to have it out with her, maybe—giving you the benefit of the doubt—to make things up. After you got over the shock of what you found, figured all the angles, you went to work.

"You didn't have anything personal against Corbeil; welcomed him, in fact. You had to have a conviction, and he was convenient, the callow college student with the girlfriend who might be pregnant. Without it, you wouldn't have an ending for your pilot episode. You said it: a show without justice won't last one season."

I looked around the large, comfortable room. "First time I saw this place, I thought of it as the house April built. She's the one responsible for your success; with a little help from you to restage the scene. If I'd only listened to myself, I'd have finished the job a lot quicker."

He was perfectly still. It was as if I was back watching him on a TV whose screen had frozen. It lasted long enough that when he opened his mouth, it made me jump in my seat.

"Heard enough?" He raised his voice a little.

I jumped, all right. I'd assumed he was alone in the house. I should have followed up by bringing the Ruger around in my hand. That would have made three guns out in the open instead of just two.

THIRTY-TWO

I'd been so caught up in Vail's absence, I hadn't considered the possibility of two men waiting in some dark room within earshot of where we sat. And when Goss called out to them I should have done something; oh, say, bring the Ruger around from behind my back. Instead I was still sitting there like a pet rock when they came in through a side doorway, armed to the gunwales.

The bigger of the two fit the profile of one of those suspicious characters that cause the police to brace them on a hunch, frisk them, and come up with an unregistered gun or a switchblade or a set of brass knuckles or maybe just a set of burglar tools. He ran a little over six feet and a little under a yard wide at the shoulders, going to fat in the middle but not enough to slow him down in a brawl, with a flat face that looked as if he'd smacked into the back of a bus. He cut his own mud-puddle-brown hair, or someone had done it for him with a pair of dull pruning shears, and if his eyes protruded any more or were set an inch wider apart he might have been part chameleon; a congenital condition, I guessed. His mother had drank or smoked or done drugs all the time she was carrying him. I don't remember what he wore. I was too busy concentrating on the spur-hammer semiautomatic in his grubby right hand to find fault with his tailor. It would fire a slug that would punch a hole through a two-inch pine board and still have enough velocity to ventilate an over-age private operative.

His companion was smaller and slighter in a baggy navy zip-front sweatshirt that hung to his thighs. It was too big for him; he'd rolled up the sleeves, but sloppily, so that the right one had crept back down to his wrist and the left was making progress against his forearm tattoos. That hand held an unfamiliar-looking pistol, an auto-loader also, in some European caliber that would probably make a smaller hole than his partner's .45, but the end result would be the same.

He had on a floppy cap drawn down over his ears, a knitted thing with multicolored stripes. I couldn't tell if he'd swiped it from Snap or Crackle or Pop.

And he looked like someone I'd met, or seen somewhere; thinner in the face, without the strong jowls, but with the same banked fury in the eyes, a kind of armor worn against the civilized world. That made him the second one I'd come across on this job, after Kenneth Whitelaw. There's no harm in failing to match faces with names—if you're a toll gate collector or a nurse in an emergency room.

Time to deal with that later. If there was a later.

Goss finished his drink and set it back down. "It's your own fault," he said. "You couldn't resist twisting the knife in me over the phone. If you'd just asked for an interview, I might not have called in my markers. That's Noble Kady there in the party hat. He didn't convert when his big brother did."

I made the connection then; if it hadn't been for the eyes I wouldn't have wondered about him at all. Brother Jared had worn a similar pair to his session with a police photographer.

"Who's his friend?"

"Company. The gun, Walker. You squirm around too much for someone who doesn't have a hunk of iron carving a hole in his back. You know how to take it out. You've seen enough surveillance footage on the show."

Two muzzles watched me like snakes' eyes as I reached back

with my left hand and brought around the Ruger, the butt between forefinger and thumb.

"Kady."

Abrahim Ibn Said's brother stepped forward to claim the revolver, pausing to ruck the restless sleeve back up to the elbow of his gun arm. I filed that away for future reference.

Goss held out his hand. Kady gave him the Ruger. He turned it over, examining it from both sides, then laid it on the table next to his glass. "Kind of gaudy for you. I'd figure you for something more modest."

"I paint my toenails too."

Kady retraced his steps and swept the foreign pistol across my face. I'd seen it coming and started to roll with the punch, but the pain shot straight through to the other side. Something trickled down into my collar, tickling my neck, and my brain was walloping off the walls of my skull as if it had come loose of the spine.

The big lunk with the bad haircut giggled. That threw me almost as much as the blow. It didn't go with his build.

"Let it bleed," said Goss, when I made a reflexive move toward the handkerchief in an inside pocket. Kady was still there close, flipping a coin whether to pistol-whip me again or save energy and pull the trigger. I let the hand drop into my lap. The blood continued to slither down my cheek and drip off the corner of my jaw.

Goss said, "That DNA evidence is nothing, just an embarrassment. I was upset when the police told me about April; my brain went into denial and I blocked out ever having been in her apartment. That visit hadn't gone well, so my conscious mind was anxious to let it go; but that's for a psychiatrist to explain. Later, when I remembered, it wasn't worth bringing up. Her killer was in custody."

He'd forgotten again just yesterday, talking to me; I let it slide.

"Embarrassing, sure." My cheekbone felt huge and hot. "Especially since you also forgot to leave any fingerprints behind except Dan Corbeil's."

"He took care of those when he wiped his off the doorknobs."

"Why bother? They were involved. He'd already marked his territory everywhere else in the place. Removing that bit of evidence was what led them to treat it as a homicide."

"You forget I'm an expert on crime. Murder is the one most often committed by amateurs. Most killers are caught because they slipped up somewhere. In this case, he compounded that mistake with trying to make it look like she killed herself: drugging her, stripping her naked, running a bath, and wearing gloves or using a handkerchief or something like that so he wouldn't leave evidence on the razor he killed her with."

"Amazing," I said.

"Not really. Not being amazing is what got him caught."

"Not Corbeil. You. You talk about your daughter's violent death as if you were dictating a letter to one of your sponsors. Your voice didn't even break when you said she was drugged and stripped and cut open."

"It was almost the last century. What's the statute of limitations on grief?"

I touched my split cheek. A lightning bolt shot straight to the top of my head, but when I took my fingers away they were sticky. The blood was slowing. "There's more," I said; "or I should say less. If Corbeil stripped her, he'd have left prints on the buttons of her blouse and the snap on her jeans."

"Wiped them off too."

I shook my head. "Forensics at the time reported finding partials on a couple of those surfaces; complete enough to identify them as April's. They weren't wiped, and if anyone had handled them, with gloves or a handkerchief or bare-handed, they'd have been smudged. The detectives overlooked that—not from incompetence, but because no case is ever clear-cut. There are always anomalies that can't be explained. Nine times out of ten, when there's a romantic interest involved, they don't need to look beyond the lover.

"You shouldn't have interfered, getting the judge to quash the evidence that April wasn't pregnant, which would have weakened Corbeil's motive. The machinery was already in place. Chances are he'd have gone to prison regardless, and I wouldn't have had a foothold that would make me reopen the investigation."

"You can't prove I had anything to do with that."

"Then why the sister act?" I jerked my head toward the gunmen.

"Insurance. There's a bare possibility Noble's brother might be compelled to explain how he tripped and stumbled into Corbeil; Corbeil himself might be able to help with that. While I thought he'd died, that seemed remote. If I bribed Jared/Abrahim to send that message, the police might look harder into the late Kenneth Whitelaw, he being a fellow *Dogs* alumnus. The way the criminal justice works, they could pile his death on top of an attempted murder charge. It seemed fitting that the associations I have that got me into this mess should be what gets me out."

I turned my head. "I got some blood on the back of your chair. You could probably sponge that out. A corpse on your carpet might take a little more than Mr. Clean."

He gave me that friendly smile he reserved for his sign-off on-screen. "Then you should have dropped by when it was still light out."

Noble Kady spoke for the first time; he had a speech impediment, a lateral lisp that made the saliva buzz between his teeth. "We got us a van in the garage; boosted it from the long-term lot at Metro. Time the owner gets back from Miami or wherever, you'll be shaking hands with Whitelaw."

"Two-car garage." I nodded. "You do luck out, Goss. Be a tight squeeze if Vail hadn't taken her car when she ran out on you. How much does she know?"

"I told you she's visiting her aunt."

"So you did. You left out her name, her Social Security number, and the name of her first pet. She's smart; that was obvious when we spoke in my office. If she doesn't know or suspect exactly what you did, the atmosphere around this place these last few days was enough to convince her you were guilty of something, and with April's case back under a microscope, she'd know it was connected. She was strong enough to go on after the death of her only child, and she's strong enough to jump ship knowing you had something to do with how it came out."

A sharp spasm in my cheek made me wince. I touched it automatically, drawing my feet back at the same moment. My center of gravity shifted forward a fraction of an inch.

"I'm no Jimmy Hoffa," I said, "but I'm not living in a refrigerator carton on Michigan Avenue either. When I'm tagged as a missing person, do you think she won't connect the dots? Maybe she remembers something from twenty years ago that would turn the whole thing up all over again, only with a ton of state-of-the-art scientific evidence to back it up. The cops won't need it, though. They'll have a fresh case of suspicious disappearance to furnish them with a whole new set of leads."

He was considering that—he wore the concerned face he used when laying out the first details of the felony du jour—when Kady grunted, a noise of impatient disgust. His loose sleeve had slid down his wrist and he raised his arm to shake it back from his gun hand.

I threw myself forward then, onto the balls of my feet, aiming a stiffened right hand at his solar plexus. It was a desperate move, and mathematically doomed to fail. I was facing two guns, not one. The big lug with the eyes of a tropical lizard aimed the .45 between my eyes and pulsed his finger on the trigger.

"Police! Drop it!"

Rhinoceros that he was, Stan Kopernick could be quiet, even when breaking down doors. He filled the entrance to the room, feet spread, pistol in both hands.

Forty-five had good reflexes for all his bulk: too good. He pivoted too fast, firing wild when Kopernick's slug tore into his chest. That made two for Kopernick: He was a double-O now.

I had the advantage of being already in motion, also of dumb clumsy luck; I recalculated my direction, dove for the Ruger on the table next to Goss's seat, managed instead to knock it off its pedestal, and goggled a little when I snatched the gun out of the air. I fired low, at Kady, hitting a kneecap; my second that week.

All this happened while Kady's partner was still falling. He twisted slowly from the hip, spiraling down to the floor with the kind of balletic grace that would have been new to his experience, if he were still in a position to appreciate it. He was through with having that luxury.

Kady was on the floor as well, grasping his knee with both hands and making a noise like a punctured tire. Ironically, the sleeve on his right arm had stayed rolled. His pistol had hit the carpet, made a lazy spin, and came to a rest against his partner's with a click. I kicked them both into a corner, purely from habit. Their owners weren't interested in them anymore.

Chester Goss stayed seated. He appeared as calm as he had all evening, except for his legs no longer being crossed and the greenish cast of his face. He didn't even raise his hands when Kopernick and I both drew down on him, and that's a knee-jerk reaction even among those who have never faced a gun. That studio calm approached paralysis.

"Got it?" I asked the detective first-grade.

"Yeah." He drew a cell phone from an inside breast pocket. "Better use it on an ambulance first."

That call having been put through, he pressed another button.

Goss's voice sounded tinny coming from the tiny speaker; he reserved his rich tones for TV.

"Insurance," it said. "There's a bare possibility Noble's brother might be compelled to explain how he tripped and stumbled into Corbeil . . ."

That accomplished what no one else had been able to achieve before; the emcee's face crumbled into a pile of confused rubble.

I took out my own cell. It wasn't as sleek as Kopernick's and had a lot fewer functions, but it worked as a telephone, which was why I got it in the first place. I broke the connection, frowned at the screen. "One bar. Wouldn't have had enough for a full confession anyway."

"We don't get 'em that often." Kopernick paused, listening to a siren pitched not as high as the wounded man's complaints. "My money's on the patient here."

THIRTY-THREE

Stop for gas?" I said.

John Alderdyce was leaning against his Taurus, hands in pockets, dressed casually for him in a maroon cashmere sweater, gray slacks, and black suede pumps with flaps over the laces.

"It's Kopernick's show," he said. "I gave him a head start. Didn't count on shooting."

"Who does?"

We watched a male-female EMS team slide Noble Kady's cot into the back of the ambulance. He was strapped in tight, and still making noise, a couple of octaves lower than before thanks to the shot they'd given him. His leg was in splints. The morgue wagon was still on its way for his partner. That particular crew is almost never in a hurry.

A Bloomfield Hills prowl car, first responder, contributed to the clutter of vehicles in front of the house. One, a deep blue steel-reinforced Mercury, I recognized from Kopernick's visit to my house. He'd run it onto the lawn when Goss's reinforcements showed up inside.

The neighbors had come out, some in robes and pajamas, to watch the show in the light from streetlamps and the thousand-candlepower spot mounted on the police cruiser. In that quarter of town they were polite enough to confine themselves to the opposite sidewalk.

I touched my cheek. The bleeding had stopped, but the throbbing went on; and I'd only just recovered from the blow to my neck. Alderdyce watched me.

"You need to have that stitched up. Al Capone could carry off the look. You can't."

"I'll take it under advisement." It came out slurred, like I was waiting for the novocaine to wear off.

"You want to tell it all here or wrap it up for later?" he said.

"Kopernick can fill you in. He's even got audio." I showed him my cell. "I ran a bluff. Now that Goss's owned up to being in the apartment, that part's sewed up tight. He said he was rattled then, but he forgot he told me about it when he wasn't."

"Hearsay; but I think we can sell it. The chief was worried about that towel. Seems probable cause and stolen evidence aren't compatible." He made a nasty chuckle. "Look at him, the big ham. Thinks he's Boston Blackie."

Kopernick, in his gray fedora and the pinstripe suit he'd ordered for his first press conference, was coming down the steps from the front door, one hand clamped on his prisoner's shoulder like an iron claw. Chester Goss, hands cuffed behind him, looked dead white in the glare of the spot. He'd left his makeup artist at the studio.

I said, "Let's hope when he makes sergeant they put him behind a desk."

"He'll find a way to fuck up even there. It's in his genetic code."

"Cut it out, John. When this is finished I mean to travel. Go someplace where the locals don't know how to spell DNA."

The detective first-grade folded Goss into the Mercury's back seat, slid under the wheel, and maneuvered the boat into the street. Alderdyce, looking after him, straightened, took his hands from his pockets, and scowled at his wrist. "Well, shit," he said. "What'll I watch now, *The Golden Girls*?"

Michael Mihalich might not have been cut out for the courtroom, but he knew how to ram through the paperwork on Dan Corbeil's release from prison. It was typed, signed, notarized, and filed before my stitches came out. The Wayne County prosecutor greased things the rest of the way. She was only too happy to clear a cell for Chester Goss.

Some penitentiaries, somewhere, probably still follow the rule of Hollywood: the big steel gate rumbles open on rollers, the freed prisoner shakes hands with a guard, and walks out into klieg-enhanced sunshine and the arms of someone waiting.

But it wouldn't be like that at Huron Valley. Corbeil would come out a plain steel door carrying his personal effects in a fat mailer. It'd be as institutional as the system itself, brief, cool, and unapologetic. I got that from Barry Stackpole when I gave him the details of Goss's arrest for his podcast. He had sources on both sides of the bars.

The embrace, if there was one, would be stiff and awkward, like the conversation during the ride home. Brother and sister were strangers after all.

That's the way it would go, more or less; I wasn't there. Chrys had invited me to the reunion, but I said it was their moment, not mine. So I stayed home to heal, catch up on my sleep, and bank my fee. I didn't shoot anyone this time.